Frances, This Time You've Gone Too Far...

Frances, This Time You've Gone Too Far...

By Janis Ost

Book design and production by
Columbus Publishing Lab
www.columbuspublishinglab.com

LCCN: 2019940432

Drawing of Frances on page 237 by Alissa Stauffer.

Paperback ISBN: 978-1-63337-298-6
E-book ISBN: 978-1-63337-299-3

Printed in the United States of America

This book is for my kids, Carina Ost and Cody Ford,
my stepson Ben Ford, and Wendy Thompson
champion teacher and colleague who says,
"Everyone gets to the door at a different rate."

In sweet memory of Jean Permison, Arthur Ost, Bob Ost,
Ileana Ost, Emily Ost, Charlie Russell,
and Joseph Tyler Clouse.

One

THERE IS ABSOLUTELY NOTHING worse than the sound of someone picking at their nails. When I tell my mom she is picking at her nails again, she says she isn't; it's just a hangnail. I guess she has a lot of hangnails. My grandmother Harriet told me to try to be nicer to my mother, especially now that we are moving from Colorado to California. Grandma Harriet signs her texts with a heart, followed by XOXOGMAH. I taught her how to text the last time I saw her. It's weird when old people text and look at their phones and smile and stuff. She's cool, but it's still weird.

We will be in Santa Cruz in nine hours and thirty-two minutes, according to my new app called *Waze*. I'm sick of the car, sick of typing on my laptop, sick of my brother humming every single Rolling Stones song, and completely and utterly sick of my mom driving with one hand while picking at her nails.

My fifth-grade teacher told me to make lists when I want to describe something. “Make bullet points,” she said. Without actually blinking, she would tell me that lists could help with clarity and a point of convergence. I can see her mousy face and large glasses, saying those words over and over again, almost like a chant. She often told me with coffee breath, “Bullet points help with details and focus. Your readers deserve clarity.” She told me that without a focal point I’d likely go into tangents and lose my audience. A part of me doesn’t care about a silly audience, but I’ve always wanted to publish a real book, so I guess I should try to please my audience, book readers, customers, or whatever you want to call them. Bottom line: lists help me, so when I unpack the boxes in my new room, I’ll find the old list and retype the descriptions of my family that I wrote recently. For the record, I’m Frances Green. I’m an eleven-and-a-half-year-old half-African-American and half-Jewish-Caucasian female who is presently on a long car trip, sitting on the brink of major changes affecting everything. For the first time in my life, my dad and I will be separated by 1,286 miles. My mom is a therapist, always asking me how I feel about stuff, but she doesn’t seem to want to hear that I’ll miss my dad. I can tell when people want to roll their eyes, even if they aren’t actually doing it. She holds a grudge that he, my dad, is in another relationship with a woman. As I am typing this, she said another negative comment.

Me: “It isn’t fair that you want me to just be nice and quiet and go along with this move without my dad.”

My mom: “Maybe he should move closer to us with his new family, that is, if Ingrid allows him to be part of his other children’s lives, you know, his older kids.”

She kind of squinted her eyes when she said this, as her eyebrows moved an inch or so upward on her face. It’s a common look I’ve identified when she feels wronged or victimized. I decided not to respond. To me, it feels like we’re throwing dirty snowballs at each other when we fight, and I figure both of us are already stressed out. Why make it worse? Only Frank, my seventeen-year-old brother, doesn’t seem agitated by being in the car for so long.

Two

WE ATE A BORING DINNER AT A DINER in West Wendover, Nevada, and stayed the night at a Holiday Inn Express. My mom said she couldn't drive any longer. My braces had been tightened right before we left Boulder, and my teeth really started hurting toward the end of the night. Sometimes I wish Tylenol cured a bad mood. I ordered macaroni and cheese and a big piece of an orangish/yellow noodle got stuck in my front wire, which put me over the edge. I doodled in my journal so I wouldn't have to look at my mom during dinner. I was trying to remember the description list I created about my family, curious if I mentioned that she says, "Are you sure?" almost every time I tell her I don't want to eat whatever is on her plate. She did it again. I looked up from my journal just in time to see her half-eaten ravioli on a fork, of course attached to her friendly hand. Why does she want me to eat her food when I have my own? Sometimes it's hard to be polite when people drive you crazy. My mom turned fifty at the beginning of July. She had a speech prepared when we threw her birthday party. There were thirteen of us at La Via Perla in Boulder, Colorado. This has always been her favorite Italian restaurant, and one of the chefs lived down the street from us so we would always get free breadsticks and spumoni ice cream. Anyway, I remember pouring oil and vinegar into this white bowl, making hearts and clouds out of this magical mixture as people stood up and said nice things about her. Afterward, she read her speech aloud. It was the first time I'd ever heard the expression "I'm having a hot flash." I thought it was weird to say in front of a group of people. My mother's face was red and she looked sweaty and vulnerable, especially while she read her odd speech. I remember asking my mom if my dad was invited to this going-away dinner.

"Do you think we should invite Dad to say goodbye at La Via Perla?" I asked in my most adult voice. After taking a gulp of coffee from her white coffee cup with the lipstick stain, she said, "Let me think about it. *No!*"

I felt bored the last few months in Boulder, but the thought of not being near my dad was making me anxious and kind of scared. Like the-first-time-I-ever-dove-into-a-pool scared. I didn't know what would happen after my feet left the diving board. You can't navigate what you can't see. It was my mom's decision that we leave Boulder. She said we all needed a change, and this was a "magical time" in all of our lives. My dad said the schools were better in California, and that the inclusion for kids on the "spectrum" was better, which would benefit Frank. Grandma Harriet said we'd get to spread out and have more room. She owns a duplex, and we'll live in one of them.

That was last month, my mom's birthday, before all of the moving boxes, before she became a nervous wreck. After she and my dad divorced, we moved and she became very annoying about everything, flipping out when I put rock band and skateboarding decals on the wall. We lived there on Birchwood Drive for almost two years. The best part of my condo—well, the condo I just moved out of—was the pool and hot tub. I became a great swimmer, winning two awards for a perfect backflip and one trophy for the butterfly stroke from swim camp. Last year, we had an all-school writing day and I wrote about swimming. Ms. Turner, the one who is obsessed with telling me to make lists, said her favorite part was when I described the back float. When and if I publish my book, I'll find my old persuasive essay on "The Joy of Swimming" and add it in.

I remember talking about the magical clouds. I said the clouds pulled me forward like a gigantic puppeteer. I feel like a puppet being pulled when I'm swimming on my back. I pretend I'm on stage and the audience can see me swim from the sky.

I never want to come into the house when I'm in the water. It's going to suck *not* having a pool, but Grandma Harriet says there are swim centers in Santa Cruz. We usually fly out to visit every year or so. The boardwalk is the bomb. I have a photo album of the four of us—Mom, Dad, Frank, and me—visiting the boardwalk when I was about eight. The arcade was giving Frank a headache. I knew this because he was covering his ears and had started humming. People were staring, but I'm used to it. The arcade is right by the beach, so I tried to walk him toward the exit to just get him outside. He wouldn't budge. His hands were stuck in his ears and he was not going to move away from the noisy machine he was standing by. I thought about the bumper cars, which were part of the amusement park, and very close to the arcade. Frank had been laughing at the people getting bumped into just a little while before we walked into the arcade. I tried to get my dad's attention, but he was busy telling Frank that arcades are fun places and was trying to distract him with a basket of French fries. Anyway, I yelled in my dad's ear, "Pick him up and take him to the bumper cars."

My dad scooped him up and the four of us walked outside the noisy arcade. I remember the smell of corn dogs and the sweet aroma of cotton candy. We all watched the swirling cotton candy being turned by a machine while an older lady smiled and handed it to a little kid. "Your sister thinks we should go to the bumper cars," he said with a raised pitch. It was as if Frank stopped freaking out that very second. His meltdown just vanished. Poof, it was gone. I was too short to be allowed on the ride, but my dad and Frank got into a bright red car and Frank got to drive.

This was the time when I knew that I had real psychic powers. I knew what people were thinking and feeling. My mom and I were watching my dad and Frankie from a table across from the bumper cars. We were dipping our fries into ketchup. Frank was crashing into other cars and cracking up. My mom said, "You know Frank better than everyone, even though you're the little sister."

I felt proud. I guess I truly am a good sister.

In about one more day, I will be able to say that I live in Santa Cruz, California. Freaky. For real. I can think of equal reasons as to why I want to and also why I don't want to move.

I promised my grandma I'd work on being kinder to my mom. I have it in writing that *If I hate it, I can live with my dad*. My mom is a therapist so I get asked questions about how I *really feel* a million times a day. Honestly, I can say that I really don't like Ingrid very much. I feel very watchful around her. She makes me feel, well, uncomfortable. I mean, she can be nice, or tries to be nice, but she's super bossy. I like her accent and how she dresses, but she thinks she knows everything about everything, and she doesn't. I will miss Chloe, but it's not like I see her a lot anyway. I will explain Ingrid and Chloe soon.

I like meeting new people, but making new friends—not so much. I have friends, but not like a real best friend. Back in Boulder, Billy Morgan is probably my best friend, but honestly, I like to be alone.

I haven't lived with my dad for more than a weekend in two years, but this will be the first time I am far away. It feels weird. That same feeling I had when I first took swimming lessons as a kid and we had a competition on the last day. We were supposed to do a cannonball dive off the board to determine our final score. I morphed myself into a pretzel, held my breath, and let my mind go blank. Bent over and shivering on the diving board, I heard people yelling, "Go, Frances!" and for a second I thought I was going to pass out with fear. I panicked that I might not be able to hold my breath long enough, nobody would find me, and I'd surely die. My nose filled up with tiny bubbles and I started coughing underwater. It was the scariest feeling I'd ever had in my life, like I had zero control. Well, I have no idea how this move is going to be. I am twitchy, scared, excited, joyful, and sad about moving, all of these feelings.

Three

JUST TO SEE WHAT WOULD HAPPEN, I put Skittles in between corn nuts and made sandwiches. I am so tired of being in this car. We are somewhere in the Sacramento area. Our car is gross and hot. The salt from the corn nuts and the dye they use to make green and yellow Skittles somehow go very well together. I used to like doodling on long car trips, but now I'd rather type on my laptop. I pretend I'm a detective gathering facts.

We went to a gas station and Frank and I got to pick out the snacks we wanted. The lights were really bright in the little store where they sold gas, and I noticed for the first time that Frank sort of has a mustache. Well, the start of a mustache. Some people say he looks blacker than white, and some say the opposite. I guess we do look related. Frank's skin is darker than mine, and his eyes are brown. I have hazel-colored eyes, just like my dad. Frank has an afro, and my hair is more poufy and crazy curly. Frank is starting to get more acne. He doesn't seem to mind, though. Lately, he's blogging about the Rolling Stones and getting a lot of hits and Twitter followers.

I remember my dad telling me about how Frank's brain works differently than my brain and most everyone else's brains. It was during my eighth birthday, and my dad was on his knees helping me with my roller skates at the roller rink while Frank was having a real meltdown. One of my skates was really hurting my foot and the laces were tied in a double knot. I couldn't untie it without help. I was missing out on my own birthday party, and Frank was busy causing a scene. He was breathing in and out really fast and his nostrils were flaring out like the wings of an airplane. My dad was watching Frank and not paying attention to my laces. Whatever he was doing to tie or untie them was actually making it worse. I hated Frank for wrecking my birthday. He was trying to win one of those dumb stuffed animals you see at the arcade, the one with the big claw that's like a crane. He put a bunch of change in the machine and nothing came out. Some skinny teenager with a shaved head and baggy pants said, "Oh, get over it!" and kind of pushed him out of the way. Frank was hysterical but didn't seem bothered at all by the kid who had pushed him. Frank didn't seem to even notice him. He was upset that he didn't get a stuffed animal.

It was a breezy day in April and we had a small party; I only got to invite a few kids. The memory is coming back clearly to me now. I was always embarrassed by his outbursts. I remember that more than the details of this birthday party.

My parents were of course still married then, and I clearly remember my parents fighting. My dad kept saying that Frank had a form of autism called Aspergers, and my mom said that my dad was obsessed with his work in the field and that Frank was simply a child who had certain interests and wasn't flexible. A common dinner scene at my house:

Mom to Frank: "Eat the food on your plate."

Frank: "No, I don't want my hamburger to touch the ketchup."

Mom to Frank: "But you're dipping your French fries into the ketchup. What's the difference?"

Dad to Mom: "Rachel, let it be."

My mom also said Frank had a bad temper due to lack of paternal attention because my dad was too busy doing research to be present and raise his own kids. He was gone too much and, as she says, she did all of the disciplining. Frank and I went to the same schools; I would see his teachers at meetings and everybody would say the same thing. "Frank is really smart, *but*…"

So, I'm the little sister to a kid in special ed. Who cares? I like when he laughs, I like when there is nothing to do and we play tic-tac-toe or just swim together. Frank can fix any computer, camera, or phone. He likes the insides of anything that resembles a machine. My mom can't even figure out how to use different parts of her vacuum, but my brother just barely glances at something broken and effortlessly puts it back together. He doesn't really care if people stare at him or tease him; he just likes the Rolling Stones and minds his own business while fixing things.

Most people don't even notice that Frank is different right away. People get it more after the second or third time they meet him. At least this is what people have told me. The expression my parents use a lot is "high functioning." Oh, and he loves California rolls, that sushi roll that has crab, avocado, and sometimes cucumber inside. He is fascinated with sushi bars, so we go pretty often. He always has to sit at the bar, though, and watch the sushi makers. He asks for their sushi knives every birthday and Christmas/Hanukkah, but my parents always tell him that you have to go to culinary school in order to buy one. Like really, why do grownups have to lie?

Me? Well I, Frances Green, am the sensitive one. My mom says she has two babies that couldn't be more different. Like I mentioned, it's very natural for me to tune into what people are thinking, and sometimes I know what people need before they even know it, kind of like when I knew Frankie needed the bumper cars to cheer him up. I have been alive here before, and my job is to take care of new humans.

It gets me in trouble because I am not afraid to say the truth. Sometimes I don't have filters.

Frances, you have gone too far. I've heard this for over eleven years.

Four

MY MOTHER IS STILL CHEWING ON her hangnails. Frank is kind of asleep, kind of awake. He has his headphones on and is listening to "Jumping Jack Flash" over and over again. My mom keeps asking me how I am. It's annoying. I know she means well. People who ask you how you are probably all mean well. But, come on, how do I answer this question when my whole life is in bags and boxes?

My dad looked sad when we had our goodbye breakfast at IHOP in Boulder. He didn't bring Ingrid or Chloe. It felt kind of like how it used to, but not really. He told me that Chloe reminded him of me when I was little, but I doubt if he remembers it. He was always at the college working. If he *was* home, he was always writing in his study with his collection of jazz music blaring. I always remember him interviewing people whose kids had Asperger's. Maybe that's why he and my mom split up. He just wasn't at home enough to be a good husband, but I mean, he had to work. If I get married, my husband will be found at home or maybe he'll even work at home. Maybe we can both be veterinarians and have our office in the back of the house.

I once went to a Renaissance festival with my parents and their friends at this big park in Denver. A gypsy lady was reading tarot cards and told me what I already knew. She said, "You are a wise soul. You have psychic abilities and people will think you are older than you are because you have been here before and perhaps remember many lifetimes."

I told her that I could read my parents' minds and also some friends'. I know I'll have a big pool and give swimming lessons as at least one of my jobs. I will also have two girls and then two boys.

So, back to my parents. I like to call them my "parental units." About two or three years ago, my dad moved out of the house. I was eight, close to nine years old. My dad was always working, like I said, and also playing tennis. My mom doesn't play, so he practiced and played matches at this gym place near the house. Because he was on the computer a lot and played tennis, he always complained that his shoulders and hands hurt, so he got massages. Ingrid worked there. I listened through the wall in my bedroom and secretly read emails and texts between my parents about Ingrid and my dad being friends with her.

It seemed like whenever I walked in the living room, my parents were fighting about this Ingrid person. “Ah geez, Rachel, we’re platonic friends, that’s all,” I heard my dad say, like a million times. Doors slammed. "Platonic" means just friends, not romantic. I googled it.

My mom tried to hide it from me, but I could tell she was miserable. My dad moved into an apartment nearby. It was a small place with gray walls and a lot of plants but very little furniture. Next thing I knew, my dad took me to Starbucks. It was during Christmas break. There was snow on the ground and it was very windy. He looked at his cell phone a lot. He seemed nervous. There was dirty snow on his boots. We were sitting at a tall wooden table and I was playing with sugar packets. Some people were singing Christmas carols, and as soon as the music stopped and the carolers left, he put his face really close to mine. I remember I had a sore neck, and I couldn’t turn it easily. It made me kind of grumpy. My dad tried to move my neck so it wouldn’t hurt. He has such soft hands. I noticed he wasn’t wearing his wedding ring. I could tell because he has cappuccino-colored skin, and the place where he usually wears a ring was a different color. My mom still wears hers. Anyway, so my dad looked at me, then back at his phone, and then said, “I have a friend I want you to meet.”

That was the day I met Ingrid. She was wearing yellow and gray exercise clothes and shook my hand in a strong way. She came to our table with wet hair and handed him something. She asked me a few questions about school and asked to see my journal I was sketching in. I always take a journal with me. I had been sketching pictures of our old dog Stella. Ingrid liked it a lot. She said so, at least.

I looked at her when she wasn't looking at me. I caught her looking at me when she thought I wasn't paying attention. Frances Green always pays attention, even when she sleeps. Ingrid Schillinger has sharp features, thick eyebrows, and big blue eyes. They are like giant marbles, actually. She has a pierced nose sporting a tiny little diamond kind of stud that you have to really look at from up close to see if it's not a speck or a freckle or something. What I really noticed about Ingrid, not to be weird or anything, was her body. She looks like a gymnast. Very thin, but strong. You kind of see a lot of her body with her clothes. She teaches yoga, so she wears a lot of those kinds of tight-fitting workout clothes and half tops. She also wears a headband. She has large, strong-looking teeth. I noticed a lot of people staring at her at Starbucks. Not a creepy stare, but more like they were looking at her the same way I was.

The next time I saw her, she was at my dad's apartment. My dad was going to pick Frank and me up and take us over to his house for dinner. My mom had one of her annoying therapist friends over and they were drinking wine at the kitchen table. My mom told my dad, who was waiting on the porch for my brother and me, to get us home early for showers and homework. It was weird that he didn't come inside the house, because it is or still was his house. Divorce is seriously awkward. So, eventually, we drove in his blue Prius to his apartment. We were making a pizza and salad. I was cutting olives, but mostly putting them on my fingers like rings or hats. Someone knocked on the door, and my dad quickly answered it. It was Miss Ingrid, again. They hugged each other, and he took her coat and hung it in the closet. She washed her hands and took out the cutting board and started scrubbing it and then put flour on it. I didn't know she was coming for dinner. I was only nine, so maybe my dad told me and I forgot. I just remember the awkward moment. My dad took the bag of pizza dough out of the fridge and was reading the directions to me.

I don't think I was mad or anything, but I remember saying, "Duh, I know how to read." It was very quiet; nobody said anything. Frank had his headphones on—as he always does—and you could hear the guitar music from the Rolling Stones.

Something in me wanted to make sure that Ingrid didn't think this was her house. I simply wanted to put her in her place. She was trying to talk to me and asked me if I had ever made pizza before. I told her that my mom buys the same dough at Trader Joe's and that she puts pineapple chunks on it. The kitchen was quiet again.

"Follow me," Dad said. The apartment had a loft with brown shag carpet in it, and I remember not really wanting to talk. I noticed that he hadn't unpacked many of his moving boxes, which actually made me forget for a few minutes that I was going to probably get in trouble for speaking my mind. I was also mad! I just felt like tuning everything and everyone out and wanted to start organizing. There was a picture in a frame sticking out of me and Frank posing with Santa Claus. My dad walked in while I was looking at this picture. He told me I was being rude and antisocial or something like that.

"But I just want to have dinner with the three of us," I told him.

He said very matter-of-factly, "I am the parent and *you* are the child."

All I could say, and I remember it like it was just now, was, "No, you are not the dad, you are a boyfriend to someone!" I yelled *someone* really loudly.

Next thing I remember, I was back at my house. My mom was putting away dishes and kept asking me why I didn't eat dinner there. This was the first time I cried, or remember crying, about their divorce. To be honest, I don't know if Frank stayed at my dad's for dinner that night. I cried until the alarm on my phone woke me the next morning for school. I was confused. I usually like new people and I knew I wasn't exactly being sweet as pie, but I didn't like this overly-friendly German lady always getting in my way when my dad was supposed to spend time with me. He hadn't told us she was eating dinner with us.

I figured it out, the part about parents that really bugs me. First, they talk too much about things and over-explain, always trying to lecture. Then, they leave out important things, like, "Hey, by the way, this lady I'm dating is going to ask you a million questions about pizza, and then try to eat it with you."

I don't remember a whole lot about the next year or so, but my dad said he wasn't used to having a small apartment and didn't care for his neighbors and also missed having his cat. So, what happened was he got a place with Miss Ingrid. She stopped coming to some of the places my dad would take me and my brother, but of course she was at their house when we went over. My mom got a condo with a pool and hot tub, and life changed. I still visited my dad regularly. I like my dad's cat a lot so I would go to their house on certain weekends. I would sit in this old rocking chair and pretend to be reading, but really I was observing what it was like at their house. One night, they were building a fire. My dad was in a really good mood and he was making these big bear noises he does when he's really happy. He kind of tickled Ingrid, and she fell over on their couch. At that very instant, I saw something that changed everything and all of our lives. Read the next chapter to find out.

Five

INGRID WAS WEARING SWEATPANTS and a workout bra with a light-blue hoodie. I always remember colors. While she was laughing at my dad's noises, and kind of did a yoga roll on the couch, I couldn't help but see her stomach. It looked like a small basketball. She must have stayed in that position for a while because her belly just stared at me. I know what women look like when they are going to have a baby. I must have been staring because she asked me to feed the cat and I couldn't move. My dad was doing a crossword puzzle on the porch. I wanted to follow him, but I was stunned. I was trying to think of a way to say or ask if she was really pregnant or if there was something wrong with her body, but all I could do was just freeze and stare. "Frances, the cat, please feed Mouse," I recall her saying. She made a sound, like an irritated sound my mother also makes, and then I imploded. My face got hot and red. I tried to talk, but I could only stutter. "Ingrid!" I yelled. I think I shouted her name a few more times. I felt like I was going down on a rollercoaster. I couldn't see anything. My heart was pounding outside of my chest. Ingrid stood up from the couch as she put her long blonde curly hair into a ponytail. It was her turn to be flustered.

I pointed to her belly. It was only the two of us in the room. Their cat named Mouse leaned up to my leg and pushed into me. Their house suddenly smelled like kitty litter. The smell made me dizzy, and then nauseated. My gaze was fixated on her belly, which was when she looked down quickly and nervously, touching the zipper of her jacket. She said in a quiet voice, and this time I could really hear her German accent, "Frances, let's get your dad over here."

I told her, "I know you're pregnant." I watched her eyes get really big. She looked scared, but also kind of happy, or excited, I couldn't tell. We locked eyes and neither of us looked away, almost like a staring contest.

"You like babies, right? You are going to be a really good big sister. We just wanted to wait and tell you…" she started to say, and then began calling out, "Kevin…Kevin, come here right now, please."

I took her hand. I held it; she smelled like fresh lemons. I never got this close to her before. For the first time, right there on the couch, I hugged her. I know I had never

ever hugged her before. She hugged me back, and unlike anything from our past, I felt like this was a secret I could be a part of. We just hugged and nobody said anything. We went to the kitchen pantry and took out the cat food and then her phone rang. She was speaking in German.

My dad returned to the kitchen and we waited for Ingrid to end her phone call. You could tell it wasn't going to be a long call because she didn't walk away. She just said, "Goo-ten ya ya ya," or something like that, and then hung up. My dad had his arm around me and said something like I was going to be taller than Ingrid soon.

"What's up, my girls?" he asked. He always shows his big white teeth when he smiles. People always say he gets his teeth whitened, but he says no, he just came out like this. He looked at Ingrid, she looked at me, and we both smiled at the same time. "Honey, she knows about the baby," Ingrid said, clutching his hand.

I suddenly felt shy. I didn't know what to say but figured they were waiting for me or my reaction. "When?" was all I could say. Then I added, "When is the baby going to be born?"

Six

I OFTEN DON'T KNOW HOW I FEEL until I start writing. I read everything I wrote since the start of the long car trip, and I don't think I did an adequate job explaining how I found out my dad and Ingrid were going to have a baby. I get critical with myself when I try to explain my Ingrid or my mom, but it's actually very daunting to capture my family with words. I get sick and tired of explaining my family, especially when they see me with Chloe. I'm forced to say, "Yes, she's my sister, but *no*, we don't share the same mom."

I feel sleepy and robotic when I have to explain this to people. The conversation is usually followed by a weird silence. It takes a lot of effort to explain complicated families. It makes my eyelids heavy.

We arrived in Santa Cruz yesterday and I've already

started making lists and drawings of where to put things. The moving truck comes tomorrow, I think, the one with all of our furniture. But let me finish telling you some things about my funny family so that you might understand how we're so complicated.

So, my dad didn't technically marry Ingrid because of some weird American or German legal document thing, but they're still engaged. She is still a German citizen, *but* they wear wedding rings, and Chloe Simone Green was born on February thirteenth, the day before Valentine's Day.

My mom and Ingrid are not the best of friends. I have tried to help them, but trust me, it didn't work. My dad called me out on telling both of them separately that the other one said really nice things about them. I guess they both confided in him, catching me in a "sort of" lie. I prefer to call it an MUP, or a "made up conversation." Ingrid probably likes my mom more than my mom likes Ingrid. Not that it really matters. I heard my mom tell some people that Ingrid just wanted to latch on to a man and stay in the United States and also that she likes married men.

After my parents got divorced, my dad got a new job at the college in Boulder. He has a PhD in Special Education, and he teaches instructors and students how to understand people who have autism. He figures out how to tap into people's skills and match them with jobs, and he's known for his articles about the inclusion of people with different learning styles in mainstream classrooms. He and Frank made a video about kids on the spectrum. My dad won some award for it. It's kind of amusing. My friends in second grade used to think that my dad was a medical doctor because people addressed him as Dr. Green.

We all went to this restaurant in Denver once with some man who designed these headphones that can drown out certain noise. You can program them so no unwanted outside noise is heard. Many people on the spectrum are sensitive to noise.

When we all lived in Colorado, we would go skiing, bowling, and to the mall like most families. We could've been your next-door neighbors. After the divorce, my parents lived in the same part of Boulder, but now it's all going to be dissimilar and unlike anything I have ever experienced this far in my melodious world. This is a new chapter in my life. My mom is by herself and she says she likes it that way. She will probably work at this place where parents bring their kids for counseling. I heard she has an interview, but they already want her to work there. I used to see a therapist named Michelle, and I will choose a new one if I decide to continue talking to someone. I try not to get anxious about stuff; that's the real reason why I had my own counselor. Usually, when everything felt fine, I would have an appointment with Michelle, and then, when everything felt sucky and I was upset, there was no appointment. I think they call it Murphy's Law. I know a lot of sayings because my mom has been a therapist all of my life. I did a history search on my mom's computer and discovered she was on a dating site called Match.com. I admit I do snoop, and besides, I'm psychic. I found out that she does want to meet people and have dates. I feel a little confused knowing this information, if you really want to know.

Seven

I'M EXCITED TO SPEND TIME WITH Grandma Harriet and also to start my new life in middle school. I'm still busy unpacking and putting things in my new room, looking forward to sleeping in my own bed again. Of course the first thing Frank did was find thumbtacks to hang his Rolling Stones posters. One thing about people on the spectrum, you might as well let them find what they like and let them enjoy it whenever they want. Frank doesn't bug me and get in my space, which is something I really like about him. As long as he has his Rolling Stones stuff, he's happy as a clam. Sometimes I listen to him by putting my ear against his door. He talks to himself a lot and interviews the Rolling Stones. I could hear him plugging in his microphone and in an animated voice he said, "Introducing Frank Green, manager of the Rolling Stones."

I don't know when he started to like them; he's just always loved them, well, for as long as I have been alive. Mick Jagger is God to him. I dusted off my mountains and mountains of books. I found and updated my description list of my family. Does everyone think they have a bizarre family, or is it just me? Here goes:

- **Mom** (Rachel Goldstein Green), fifty years old
  - Her ancestry is Russian/Jewish
  - Small frame, short brownish/grayish curly hair, glasses, doesn't rub her makeup in very well
  - Marriage/family therapist
  - A nice person, worries about everything

- **Dad** (Kevin Green), fifty-two years old
  - African American, tall
  - Most people say handsome, hazel eyes, perfect teeth
  - Professor at the University of Colorado in Boulder, Colorado
  - Specializes in special education and inclusion models
  - Mostly cool (but forgets promises), loves tennis
  - Engaged to Ingrid (it's a long story)

- **Ingrid** (stepmother, sort of), thirty-four years old
  - German, pretty, bossy, yoga instructor/massage therapist

- **Chloe** (almost stepsister), two years old
    - Cute, curious, breaks my things

- **Grandma Harriet**, seventy-eight years old
    - Gray hair, widowed, really into women's rights, wears purple, funny, retired artist

- **Frank Green** (brother), seventeen years old
    - Has Asperger's Syndrome (kind of autism), a whiz with computers
    - Biracial, wears glasses, mostly quiet, walks very fast, obsessed with The Rolling Stones

And…last but not least, me:

- **Frances Green**, eleven-and-a-half years old
    - Tall, hazel eyes, biracial (that's what my school file says)
    - Excellent swimmer, psychic, organized, writer/poet

As I set up what will be my new life, I see my mom from the front window, opening and closing the trunk of her car. She seems to be looking for something, probably her cell phone. My teeth hurt again. I guess I have to find a new orthodontist. The one I went to in Boulder was named Dr. Lee. He is Chinese and was born in Peking. He speaks with a slight accent and tells jokes. This is his favorite joke:

Q: When is it a good time to go to the dentist?

A: Tooth-hurty.

He kind of says it to everyone, and then he laughs and says, "Get it?"

I think I'll miss him. The ladies in his office gave me a lot of envelopes filled with bands and told me to take pictures of all the movie stars and to enjoy California. I tend to like dental hygienists more when I'm not in their chair. I feel like they turn on me. Here's how: they act really friendly when they see you. "Oh, hi, Frances. What a cute jean jacket you're wearing. Hope you're having a nice summer."

They start to clean your teeth and they tell you ever so gently that you should work harder on keeping your teeth and gums clean with braces. You nod your head because there are tools and instruments in your mouth, and obviously you can't talk. They claim that they all had braces at one time or another, and they totally admit how hard it is to brush effectively. Everything is going well, and then the dentist comes. The scene changes dramatically. They mimic whatever the dentist says and find fault with your brushing, which crushes me because I want to be good at everything. It's not good to have any pocket higher than a "three." Oh crap. My gums even bleed sometimes. They measure your pockets and I pretend that my teeth are very expensive and symbolic relics from the past, and the higher the number, the more money they are worth. I like visiting the dentist until you get into that awful chair. It's awkward and embarrassing but I'm sort of obsessed with teeth, so it's worth it. It's freaky to think that when you move, everything changes, even your orthodontist, friends, teachers, libraries, blah blah blah.

When we pulled up in front of our new home, Grandma Harriet was sitting on the porch with her Yorkie poodle named Lola. She came running out to the car to greet us. Harriet has short gray hair and a really friendly smile. Her voice is very deep and she organizes protests and marches. I have seen many pictures of her in marches, holding up signs, and Lola is in every picture. She likes to hug people and talks to everyone in her New York accent. The duplex is painted gray with red trim. It has three small bedrooms and two bathrooms.

That night, she cooked us a tasty chicken and wild rice dinner and then sat on my bed with Lola, who goes everywhere my grandmother does. My grandmother is a little lonely, very original, and gives me a lot of attention. My art is all over her house; she saves everything. She gets into it with my mom because she thinks my mom worries too much about things. Grandma Harriet is right; my mother is a worrywart.

I was putting my rubber bands in, on my braces, of course, as we talked about places to hike in Santa Cruz. My mom walked in, asking if we could call her phone. She won't say she can't find it, she just says, "This move has me a little absentminded." My grandma and I were making funny faces behind her back, which she didn't see. We like to tease my mom about being disorganized. I guess I have the opposite brain. I'm really good at lists, putting things in order, and have always been incredibly organized. My conversation with Grandma Harriet this morning:

"Your mother is under a lot of pressure, Frances."

"I know. And I just moved almost 1,400 miles."

"Yes, but you are young."

"I'm mature for my age."

"I know."

"Your mother should join Jewish Singles. She deserves a nice, decent gentleman caller to take her to dinner. She works very hard, you know."

"I noticed she was looking at home."

"Home?" she asked.

"Home," I replied.

"Home? Frances, you talk in code. What is looking? Where is home?"

"In Boulder," I said.

"Home is here. I am your home."

"My dad isn't here, so it isn't home."

"Your dad cares for you, I'm sure, but he has a new family. The Goldsteins, they stick together. You'll be happy here, trust me. Your mother though, oy vey. Who was she looking at, your mother?"

"Men. An online dating site, Match.com, I think. Don't tell her anything, please. They looked old."

"Were they Jews?" she asked, giving me a serious face.

"How should I know?" I replied.

"I can always tell. I can always tell."

My grandmother often says things twice. What I didn't say was that besides losing things, my mother also gets distracted. She starts one thing and then forgets to finish. She was making tea and talking on the phone one day. The teakettle was whistling loudly. I yelled "Mom" from my room, and then the whistling stopped. She was on her computer screen typing something and then started yelling, "Frank, are you hungry?" but she kept typing and didn't wait for an answer.

I walked to where she was and told her that he probably couldn't hear her. I saw a photo of a man with grayish hair sitting on a boat. This is how I knew she was on a dating site. His name was Gary. She was squinting and putting on different pairs of glasses, unaware that I was also reading what was on the computer screen.

I told my mom she should make something for Frank to eat because he is getting pimples and not eating enough healthy food. She touched my cheek in a loving way and told me I was right and walked away, probably going to Frank's room or somewhere in that vicinity. This was my chance. I took the chair she had unintentionally warmed for me and started reading the site. I discovered that you can wink at people and the person posting their ad can see this wink.

I knew she'd be distracted once she arrived in Frank's room. She would have to compete with the Rolling Stones playing in my brother's ears. She would ask him what he wanted to eat and he would answer that he doesn't know. Then she'd ask him the usual questions, you know: hot or cold, sweet or savory?

I figured I had a good five minutes. I proceeded to look at a bunch of single men in their forties, fifties, maybe sixties. She was looking in the zip code area of Santa Cruz, which meant she was planning to meet them there, or was at least curious. I did a quick search for wealthy men but nothing came up. I found a few men in the Santa Cruz area, including the guy with the boat named Gary that had my grandma's same zip code, and started winking. My mom yelled out that nobody could decide on food. I hollered back, "I'm hungry but don't know for what."

She then yelled out, "We'll have Chinese food delivered. Where is my purse? I need my credit card!"

I figured this was good news; I had more time to wink. Obviously, she would be looking for her purse for another few minutes. I admit I took this little prank a little too far, but before I knew it, I winked at three or four dozen single men. I like meeting new people, and if it were up to my mother, she would just stare at them and read what they had to say and do absolutely nothing.

When I was done, I just shut the computer down and read my Jerry Spinelli book. My mother would forget she was logged onto the computer anyway. Frances leaves no traces. When in doubt, put your face inside of a book and nobody will suspect you of anything.

Eight

IT'S BEEN A GREAT WEEK; I FOUND A place to swim and met a few neighbors. My mom started her new job at the Parent's Center, and Frank is setting up high-speed internet in our house and also at Grandma's. Did I say that Grandma Harriet owns this duplex?

The best part of my week was when my grandma and I walked to a gym that she belongs to. It's also right down the street from my school. Everyone assumes I'm older because I'm tall. Everyone assumes I'm in a higher grade than I am because I like to use words like "preposterous" and "enigma." The front desk person at the gym named Ted, a blond guy who looked like a surfer, said, "Oh, Harriet, I see the resemblance. This must be your granddaughter from Colorado you talk about."

Grandma used to tell people that I'm the better-looking

one with the super tan skin. An older, very athletic lady with a clipboard signed some papers and welcomed me on my grandma's family membership. She asked, "Which high school do you go to?" She thought I was a freshman! My grandma just winked at me and said, "We're still deciding."

I feel really proud to belong to a gym. The pool is perfect for my laps. There are some cute little kids who live across the street from the gym that I might babysit. I talked to their mom Phoebe, who is a hairdresser. The only other Phoebe I've ever heard of is Holden's sister in *The Catcher in the Rye*. How cool is that to really meet someone with that name? Anyway, she has short brown hair and wore cute shorts with fringes. She had flip flops on and bright red toenail polish on her toes. She said, "I really like your hair, it's killer!"

I was wearing a headband, and it was just down. Some people assume I am a light-skinned black girl, and others think I am Caucasian mixed with Latina, unless they see my hair natural and I don't straighten it. I like that it's different. Frank has more of an afro than I do, but I do have a lot of hair. His eyes are dark brown, and mine are kind of light green or hazel, as I mentioned. You know, like my dad's.

My mom seems to like her new job and is not nearly as stressed as when we were packing and driving out here. I miss my dad. We FaceTime or text about every two days, but it feels weird not seeing him, as if there is a long tunnel separating us. I wonder if he misses me. I mentioned that to my mom, who of course said this was an "opportune time to find a therapist."

She took me to a place on Seabright Street close to the ocean. The therapist was an older woman named Shirley Tinsdale, who wore artsy glasses and big rings on her small, salami-shaped fingers. She had thick, gray hair with super short bangs and she nodded her head nervously. We made small talk for about ten minutes, you know, to see if it was a fit. When I met my mom near the front door after she filled out some paperwork, I said, "No, Mom. Michelle was cool. This lady is not cool. I can't pick her."

A few days later, we rode our bikes downtown and then walked upstairs on these long wooden stairs leading to a cozy office overlooking downtown Santa Cruz. Most mothers take their daughters clothes shopping, mine takes me therapist-shopping. A really friendly lady named Joanie came out to the lobby and offered us ice water with lemons. She had bright turquoise eyes and super wavy blonde hair, with gentle hints of gray. I liked her vibe. She wore a scarf and jeans and lots of silver bracelets. I resonated with her art in the hallway and enjoyed the acoustic music playing in the background.

My mom stayed in the waiting area. I followed Joanie into a small room with cinnamon-colored walls. We talked alone in this office for a few minutes, mostly about Boulder and if I liked Santa Cruz so far or not. Her full name is Joanie Van Brundt, and I immediately felt an energetic connection to her. She smiled when I told her that. I asked, "When can we get started?"

"I see a lot of teens, but we'll work you in," was her response.

My mom said her insurance will kick in soon and I can see Joanie every two weeks if I want. I felt safe and comfortable in her office. I kind of wish I could just hang out there and sketch or write poetry. Something tells me that Joanie and I will be psychic with each other.

Today, I stayed in my pajamas all day and read a lot. My room was too quiet; I needed to break the silence. I called Billy. He asked if I made friends yet. I said, "I want to make some friends, but I think girls my age are pretty mean. To be honest, they bore me. Half the time when my friends talk about stuff, I just daydream because I couldn't care less. Girls my age care too much about looking pretty. They look in the mirror constantly, and they're conceited and snotty. Well, they *can* be mean and snotty, as my mom would say."

Billy responded with, "That sounds rough. Just be yourself I guess." I think I heard a video game or the TV in the background; he seemed kind of like he didn't want to talk on the phone. We said we'd talk another time and we hung up. I felt defeated somehow. I took a long hot bubble bath and jotted down these words afterward on the notes app on my phone:

I get good grades because I work hard, and I'm tall, so people always think I'm older. Maybe teachers expect more from me, so I don't want to disappoint them. I read *Are You There God? It's Me, Margaret* when I was ten because I already got my first period. I reread it many times because if I write a book, I want to write for preteens and teenagers. I don't know why, but when I try to be nice to girls my age, they give me funny looks. Boys are just easier to hang out with. They have way less drama. It doesn't mean I have crushes on them, it just means they're a lot more fun to hang out with. They don't change how they treat you when other people are around like girls do. My mom said just be kind to girls like this and they'll know I'm a nice person. No thanks. I don't want to waste my energy on girls like that.

Sometimes I wish I could just switch into college and skip middle school and high school. We live near the middle school I'll be attending, and I hear it's a good school. My grandma used to volunteer in the art class. She used to be a high school art teacher. She

said all the girls she met at the middle school were very sweet. Kids always act differently when grownups aren't around, though. That is something old people have to learn. I don't think my grandma is aware of that.

I think I should write a book about being a female preteen in America. Someone who isn't "white." Someone who has a brother that everyone kind of knows but nobody really understands. Someone who has a dad but has to be cool with the fact that her dad also has a new family and lives in a different state. Someone who has a mom that helps repair relationships but is actually divorced and can never find her purse or her phone, AND picks at her nails and skin, driving you absolutely crazy.

The book will describe what it's like to feel like an outsider. What it feels like to always feel a little anxious because you're always alert and observant. Your different nature causes insomnia, because the pulse of life is in your mouth, your head, and body, and so often you can't close your eyes. The book will

be for people who were born feeling like an adult and don't have the patience to be a teenager. It's so hard to grow up when you already know stuff, but can't prove it.

I might work these thoughts into a poem. When I have an appointment with Joanie, I'll likely bring these ideas in for her to see if she understands.

Nine

I WAS PICKING MINT FROM THE GARDEN and sweeping when a mom and her kid stopped me. I took off my headphones and stuck out my right hand for a handshake, just the way my parents taught Frank and me. "Frances Green," I said automatically. The mother's name is Leslie and she's a nurse and knows my grandma. She's really pretty, with shoulder-length blonde hair and bright blue eyes. She said to me, "I heard great things about you. Would you like to babysit my kids sometime?" I told her I would, and her little girl started touching my bracelets.

"Your grandmother said you're really good at organizing. I could use your skills. My kitchen is a disaster. I'll pay extra," she said while holding her little daughter, who was now grabbing my bracelets, trying to take them off. It made us all laugh.

I enjoy going to people's houses; I have always been curious about people's personal lives. When I look inside people's houses, I like to imagine a system to organize their things, and if there isn't one, I'll for sure create it. Picture a bookshelf. Any size will do. Now picture all kinds of books on it, falling over. The bookshelf is ugly and disorganized. I want to jump out of my skin when I see chaos.

So, the Frances method, or system, is to take everything off. I use Clorox wipes or Dawn soap in a bucket and put on music, cleaning the bookshelf thoroughly. Step two, I put the hardcover books with hardcover books and softcover books with softcover books. Next, I organize them by color. Usually, people have more paperbacks than hardcovers, so I put them stacked up, the biggest ones on the bottom. I start with red, for no reason. Then blue books, then green, then yellow and orange, then brown, then white and black together. It usually ends up looking really cool.

Leslie called me and suggested that I come over with my grandma, who already knows her children. We made a plan that she'd stay a little while, and then leave when the kids felt okay with just me.

Her kids are really cute and pretty easy. We drew some pictures and watched *101 Dalmatians*. They fell asleep during the movie, so I opened up the pantry and saw mayhem. Things were spilled out everywhere, cracker crumbs sprinkled over upside down cans and boxes of Jell-O on the floor. I imagined how cool it would be to be a grown up and have my own closet with cans of olives and taco shells and tuna and all of these things that this family did.

It took me about an hour to take everything out and organize it. I just put all of the snacks together, neatly stacked all baking items on one shelf, and organized cereal and oatmeal and breakfast kind of food on another shelf.

Leslie came home and seemed really happy. The kids woke up when she was talking to me. She asked if I could babysit the upcoming Friday night. I put it on my calendar and later told my family how well it went.

The next Friday, Leslie made us dinner and left while we were drawing pictures. Her kids didn't even cry! We played with Legos and read books. Caitlin, the little girl, wanted her hair in French braids, so I was happy to do it for her.

I texted with my dad for a little bit, but I didn't want to be on my phone when the parents came home, so I just started organizing the kids' art paper and pens when they walked in. The kids fell asleep on their sleeping bags in the living room.

They gave me $25 and seemed really chill. They smelled like garlic and wine and they carried their kids like little bundles from their blankets on the rug to their bedrooms. Today, I'm really stoked that we moved here. It feels fantastic to be paid for something that's so easy. I also know for sure that I want to have kids one day, at least four of them.

Ten

"FRAN, DO YOU WANT TO WALK TO the gym?" my mother asked as we were putting away the dishes. I was actually doing the work. She gets distracted, remember? I could tell she wanted to talk to me. She hardly goes to the gym, but when she does, she just likes the pool and reads her books on the stationary bike. She gets hangnails at the gym too, if you know what I mean. My mother is a nervous picker. You might think I look at her all of the time. I look at her peripherally. I'm a writer. It's my job to watch people.

I agreed to go to the gym with her, so we put on our exercise clothes and headed out. Frank was taking a rest in his room.

The gym is only a few blocks away. We passed the donut place on the way. The smell was incredible. I love the smell of donuts baking, especially old-fashioned glazed donuts. It's the most satisfying smell in the whole world. My mom was making funny faces with her mouth. She kind of bites the inside of her lip when she is nervous or is thinking about how to say something. I can always tell. Like my grandmother would say, "I can *always* tell."

"Your father and I have been divorced for over three years, Franny. How do you feel about—"

I cut her off. "About you dating?" I offered, as I helped her readjust the gym bag she was starting to drop on the ground.

She looked like a shy teenager. "Well, kiddo, good guess. That's pretty much what I was going to say."

"It's fine, Mom. It's your life," I said as we walked into the gym and signed in with the jocks at the front desk. They were asking us how our day was, and the music was loud. A lot of people were walking out as we were walking in.

She obviously wanted to talk more because she stopped walking. We hadn't even made it to the locker room yet. My fifty-year-old mother needed me; it was written all over her face. She not only picks at her nails, but she also picks at these things on her face. She is sensitive about it, so I tried to look away. She told me once when I saw her with tweezers, staring at herself in front of her bathroom mirror that they weren't "pimples," but rather ingrown hairs on her chin. Well, she covers them up with a shade of foundation that is obviously too dark. It bugs me. She doesn't blend it in right. I notice colors, especially when things aren't blended. It feels like an itch I can't scratch. I tried to help her once, but she yelled at me, "The bathroom is my only privacy. O-U-T, I say!"

On this particular morning, I was okay with my mom wanting to talk, but that little island of powder, dark foundation, and a trace of blood sticking out on her chin grossed me out. I could tell she'd been picking at it too. I told myself to try to focus on her eyes. Her eyes have always reminded me of a tired owl, but a kind of nice tired owl.

I couldn't stop looking at her chin, so I suggested we walk to the pool area. There is a little bench between the pool, hot tub, and the steam rooms, and we sat down. We were both kind of watching the swimmers and an older couple in the hot tub.

"Well, what do you think about me making new friends here?" she asked again, this time in a softer voice.

"It's your life," I repeated.

She got a bit louder. "When you say that, you're not really saying your opinion."

I wasn't going to let it end there. My response came out really fast, "Guess what? When I give you my opinion, it hurts your feelings. I can't win."

I was proud of how it sounded. Our conversation ended abruptly. We studied each other's faces, saying nothing. It became very clear. She actually *invites me to hurt her feelings.*

Her face looked kind of sad, her gaze was down, and she was fiddling with her fingernails. "Let's both make new friends here, okay, Mom?" I offered, sort of putting my arm around her.

"Male and female," she said.

"Yin and yang," we say in unison. I learned that expression about balance in the universe when I was about ten years old.

When I looked at her gain, she had a slight smile on her face, just a sliver of a moon. Now her tired owl eyes looked a little perkier. She told me that she has decided to take on new challenges and become braver since the move. In a very business-like kind of way, she added, "Frances, again I repeat, this includes making friends with the opposite sex."

I suddenly felt like swimming and doing exercises, not talking. I started to stand up, and she stopped me. "Oh, there's one more thing I keep forgetting to ask. Did you happen to get on my computer and fool around with my emails when we were still in Boulder, I mean, before we moved? You have, you know, invaded my privacy in the past."

About a year ago, I found out that you could order books from Amazon Prime and have them delivered in two days. I was aware that my mom had her account set up, so I ordered some Jerry Spinelli books. She got upset that I logged on to her account without asking. I hardly call that "invading her privacy," but whatever.

I felt a hot blob slowly crawl up my neck like a caterpillar as I took a deep breath, shook my head, and flatly told her, "No." All of the noises from this crowded gym distracted me and I was forced to look, once again, at the gross island of makeup on my mom's chin. This was now super bugging me. I just *had* to wipe it off, rub it in, or blend it in better. My heart began to beat really fast. I didn't think she would ever ask me this.

"Why do you ask?" I asked.

She looked confused. "One person I've been corresponding with thinks that I noticed him first. You know, as in initiated things. He told me so. That's all. Never mind." She looked nervous, threw her hands up, and said sweetly, "Forget I said anything, darling."

As soon as she was out of my sight, I jumped in the pool. While I did laps, I thought about how I would be judged for lying to my mom if there really is a God. I don't like to lie, I *really* don't, but my mother needed my help. She just did realize it. I was probably her mother in a past life.

I wonder how my mom feels about my dad having a family besides Frank and me. My dad never asks about how she's doing, he just tells us to respect her and that she's a good mom. When Chloe was born, my mom got my dad and Ingrid a baby gift, but she doesn't go inside their house and seems *very* awkward when we see them at different places like birthday celebrations and holidays. I jumped out of the pool, got a drink of water from my bottle in my gym bag, and returned to do more laps. I tried to distract myself by imagining what middle school would be like, as well as visualizing the last chapters of math I'd been learning in fifth grade. I decided to flip over. All these memories from Colorado came flooding back to me.

Suddenly, as I was doing my treasured back float, my head bumped into something. My mom, who'd been waiting at the end of the pool, abruptly grabbed my neck to get my attention. It totally caught me off guard. I wanted to yell at her but felt guilty for getting into her personal stuff online, so I said nothing. Anyway, she said, "Franny, it's getting late; let's walk back."

She kept on looking at her cell phone on our walk home. There is a feeling in my chest when my heart pounds really fast, an indicator that I'm holding a grudge, or mad or worried, and frankly I don't like it. I made myself think about other things, like opening up a bank account and saving babysitting money. I figured I could charge more per hour because I also organize people's homes. We walked past a beautiful maple tree. I was taking a picture in my mind because I wanted to paint a still life watercolor of the unusual leaves. My mood switched before my eyes. It's so empowering to be mindful, to decide how you want to feel, and then have the power to raise your mood and your feelings. I watched the sky change colors, from dark gray to turquoise.

I suddenly felt like something great was about to happen, that I was somehow exactly where I should be. I remember telling my mom at this moment, "I'm glad we moved, and I love you."

Some skateboarders cruised past us as we hugged. My mom looked like she had a tear in her eye. She grabbed my hand tightly and told me, "This means a lot to me, thank you. I love you to the moon, kiddo."

With a sudden mischievous grin on her face, she said, "Last one to the house is a rotten egg," and she started running.

I yelled back, "Look out, there's dog crap!" and pointed to the curb she was just ready to step on. She stopped running, completely coming to a halt. It was at that precise moment that I took off with full speed, running as fast as I could. As I ran, I felt deliriously happy. Free. We were only a block away from the house, and I could hear my mom laughing, combined with the sound of her tennis shoes scraping the pavement. I hopped over the hose on the porch and pushed the door open, laughing in a way I hadn't in a long time, landing on the living room couch. Frank was watching a Rolling Stones special on the TV. He said, "What's so funny?" A few seconds later, my mom, out of breath, came sprinting in the house. She threw her workout towel on top of my face and called me a punk.

Frank told us, "Hey, you guys are loud and silly." He

looked annoyed. This, of course, made us laugh even harder. Frank has a way of squinting, like he is looking straight into the sun, when things frustrate him. When I got out of the shower later that day, my mom was eating yogurt and looking at her computer. She motioned for me to come closer. She had a big smile on her face. "Frances, what do you think about your mother meeting a veterinarian who wrote a book about the behavior of dogs?"

I studied her face. She was scraping the side of the yogurt container even though there was no yogurt left. She looked like some friends I have when they have crushes on people.

"Does that mean we'll get a dog if you like him?" I asked.

I suddenly had a lot of questions. My curiosity was lit up like a nighttime carnival ride.

I know people meet each other on dating sites, but I don't really get how it works. My mom counsels couples and helps with relationships, so I figure she knows some things. I focused my eyes on hers and pretended that my ears were really tape recorders.

What if one person likes the other one more than they are liked? What if neither person likes the other? What if they both like each other? How long is the first meeting? I wanted to ask my mom all of these questions, but I also know that when I start dating, I don't want her to ask me anything.

I said, "Mom, how long does the first meeting last?"

She gave me a funny look. "Well, Frances, I'll have to time it."

She proceeded to tell me, "I'm going to meet someone for coffee later in the afternoon."

I said, "Where?"

I suddenly felt a nervous feeling in my gut, kind of like a shooting cramp. She answered, "Downtown," and then basically walked to the kitchen and started doing dishes, acting like it was no big deal. I noticed for the first time that she was not wearing her wedding ring. She used to almost always wear it, even after they divorced. She would tell me that people talk too much in small towns like Boulder, and she didn't feel like airing out her personal life.

I know my mom asks a bunch of questions, because for one thing, I have talked to counselors and therapists before, and another thing, I have heard her talk to clients on the phone. I sometimes listen to her from my room, and recall her often saying, "Tell me more."

I listen to my parents' conversations over the phone whenever possible. My mom almost always puts *all* of her calls on speakerphone, except when she talks to clients. Come to think of it, they are getting along better than they used to. I hear them say "fair enough" a lot. Some of my initial memories of when my dad moved out are getting foggy. It's kind of like a dream that you can remember only sections or parts. My dad did spend time with Frank a lot, and they played *Guitar Hero* and video chatted. I have memories of playing chess at Billy Morgan's and watching music videos. I took a lot of naps with my dog, Stella. Sometimes I would spy on my mom and pretend to be asleep on the couch so I could hear her talk to her friends on the phone.

My mom is both private and social. I don't like when she talks about my dad to other people. I asked her to keep it to herself because she used to talk too much about their divorce, like how she feels about Ingrid. "Thank you for sharing your feelings with me. I will be aware of your request." She said this in a very formal tone, as if she was answering the phone at a complaint department. I think my parents get along better than a lot of people I know with divorced parents.

I did listen in on a call between my mom and my grandma last Christmas. Well, my mom had it on speaker, and I was studying my CPR pamphlet, so I couldn't help but hear. My problem is that I can see everyone's side in many situations. My mom said that Kevin, my dad, always paid a lot of attention to other ladies and that he wasn't home with us when we were young. I guess he was published a lot and traveled around talking about Asperger's and, as she put it, my mom was the one at most of "our son Frank's" special education meetings, not him, even though he was the "specialist." She always says "specialist" in a sarcastic way when she is referring to my dad. She would cock her head to the side and look kind of like an angry cartoon character. I remember my grandma not saying too much, but she did say he acted selfish, which made me feel kind of sad, and she also said more than a few times, "Oh Rachel, move closer, I can help."

I can see my grandma's side because my dad was gone a lot, and now he has a new person in his life and my mom does not. I have overheard her telling my mom that even on their wedding day he had a wandering eye. My grandma is just trying to protect my mom. I guess it doesn't really matter how old your kids are, you probably always want to see them happy. She doesn't really talk badly about anybody, which is something I admire.

I can see my dad's part too, because he is a good person and really likes to help others. He is also a respected professor at a good college, teaching others about being on the spectrum. Like I said, he works a lot. Not to sound mean, but my dad acts younger than my mom even though he's older. He goes to parties, always dresses up for funny things on Halloween like Albert Einstein and Frankenstein, and once Marilyn Monroe. He plays tennis, jogs, and goes to the gym. My mom is more of a couch potato. She likes to watch shows about singers and comedians auditioning and old episodes of *Friends*, *The Office*, and other shows that make her laugh. She gets emotional when people are voted off shows like *The Voice*, and I have also witnessed this with some cooking shows. I swear she is the most sensitive person in the whole world. The picture I have of my mom in my head is of her sitting on the red leather couch with our dog, Stella, wearing her Uggs and, of course, nervously picking at her nails. Stella died at the beginning of fifth grade, but I don't want to think about it. The picture of my dad in my head is a split screen of a tennis player and a light-skinned black man listening to jazz and reading books on autism. I wonder if I will always be able to see everyone's sides when people divorce.

I thought about my funny mother meeting some random guy for coffee. I think she would do better if I was there. I'm fine with my mom meeting a friend for a coffee date; I just feel, I don't know, a little weird about it.

I went back to my neighbor Leslie's house and organized her kitchen drawers, saucepans, and cooking things. I made $20 in about two hours and came to the realization that I feel calm when I organize things. I'm good at creating order.

My grandma returned to my house and brought us tomatoes and cilantro from the garden. We made salsa together and teased my mom as she was getting ready. She would put on jeans, look in the mirror, say, "Oy vey," and then try on other pants, at least three different dresses, and two sweaters.

She put lipstick on, and then took it off. My grandma suggested that she would take Frank and me out so that my poor mother wouldn't feel nervous. Frank likes to drink coffee, so we decided to go to Peet's Coffee downtown. It was cloudy out for a summer day. The sky seems lower than it does in Boulder. We parked by the movie theatre and Frank was reading the movie titles out in front of the theatre. My grandma was trying to hurry us into the coffee place. I can tell she doesn't like to disappoint Frank. This is what I mean about being psychic. I can just read people so easily. We told Frank we were going out for hot chocolate and coffee, not a movie. Frank stared at the marquee and said, "*Chef*, let's see *Chef* please."

Next thing I knew, my grandma was texting my mom to let her know we would also see a movie. We got our tickets for the next show and then went to Peet's Coffee to get drinks. I thought about my mom and hoped she would have a good date. My mom is a terrific listener. She gets people to talk about personal things by listening. I hoped this guy would let her talk. I worry sometimes that she doesn't do what she wants to do because she listens to everyone else's point of view. I mean, everyone should, I guess, at least a little bit, but she goes overboard. She thinks I'm bossy, but I'm just really good at making up my mind and she isn't. I think God, or whoever makes mothers and daughters, creates them completely opposite so that it becomes like a really hard college class all families with mothers and daughters are forced to take.

Chef was a fun movie about a dad who loses his job at a fancy restaurant and starts his own business with a used food truck. His son gets to travel around with him. Frank said he liked it and wanted to go home and make a grilled cheese sandwich. It felt good to have family time. My brother doesn't always want to go out on the weekends, and since we moved, it seems he hasn't made any friends. Back in Boulder, my dad helped him start a group with other kids who have Asperger's. He doesn't usually call his friends to hang out, but the parents of other kids with Asperger's set up play dates with bowling, pool, and restaurant parties. They would all meet in restaurants, bowling alleys, and go on walks and trick-or-treat together, and stuff like that.

When we got home, we immediately grabbed the salsa we made from the fridge. We put some tortilla chips in a bowl and pigged out. Frank buttered the pan, just like the dad in the movie, and the three of us polished off really delicious, extra cheesy grilled cheese sandwiches. The sky got dark and I realized my mom was gone a long time. I sent her a text: *Having fun, Mom? When are you coming home?* No answer. I called her and it went straight to voicemail. What nerve!

Eleven

MY GRANDMA DECIDED TO GO BACK to her house, which is, of course, right next door, and Frank went to his room to probably Skype with our dad or watch a Rolling Stones interview. I realized I was now that thing I like, but actually don't like. I was alone. I remember when my parents split up, I would beg both of them not to call a babysitter for me. I wanted to be grown up. My dad was less protective than my mom. He just doesn't worry about half of the bad things that can go wrong like my mom does.

I prefer to be alone when I am at one of their houses, but then once I am alone I can feel either of two things. I feel like I can do anything, and I plan things. I feel grown up, brave, smart, and free. Other times when I am alone I feel, well…lonely. Different. Awkward. Insecure. Not completely African American or Caucasian. Too tall, too smart, bored with things that kids my age like. Boy crazy, but shy if a guy stands too close. Clumsy. Weirdly good at organizing. OCD perhaps. I read about the characteristics of OCD and I'm sort of like those people. All of these things I like about being different are the same things I don't like about myself, in a hot and cold kind of way.

I thought about this stuff so much that I gave myself a headache. I was definitely in the "not good" lonely zone. I felt like I was going down the rabbit hole in *Alice in Wonderland*, which I read when I was in the third grade. I thought about my third-grade teacher and the day we all stopped doing math centers because she said our class should watch the snowfall instead. I started missing my dad, and Chloe, and maybe even Ingrid. I thought about Stella, our old rescue dog, and before I knew it I started to feel hot tears coming. I looked at my phone. My mom had not answered my texts or returned my phone calls. I called my mom again, no answer, just her outgoing message.

I must have dozed off because I was drooling a little and I woke up to the sound of tires on gravel. I remembered seeing headlights on my bedroom wall.

I heard a door open and close, and finally she burst through the door singing some Bob Dylan song. I heard her throw the keys down on the kitchen table (I told you she always loses them) and then she walked into my room. She put the light on and it hurt my eyes.

"Hey, turn it off!" I found myself saying in an irritated tone. I told her, "I didn't appreciate being ignored!" as I lay down on my stomach so she couldn't see my face.

She said, "I wasn't ignoring you."

I asked her, "Why didn't you return my texts or my phone calls?"

She answered, "It is rude to look at your phone when you are meeting someone for the first time."

"Well, what would have happened if your own mother had a heart attack or if Frank would have choked on popcorn?" I added in a loud voice, "Clearly, your new Santa Cruz boyfriend is more important than your own family!" I blurted it out sharply as I turned over, staring straight into her pupils. I couldn't control my tears. They flowed down my cheeks like an angry river. She just hugged me.

"Oh, Frances," she started…

"Are you getting remarried, Mom?" I had to ask her.

"Frances…" she repeated, holding my hands in hers.

We said the following words together: "This time you've gone too far." For some reason, I started to laugh, then I cried, then I laughed some more.

Twelve

FRANK GOT A PART-TIME JOB AT Best Buy. He basically helps customers figure out which kind of computer and printer they would benefit from choosing. His Workability teacher from his high school helped him with the application and interviewing process. He seems to be really happy about his new job. He wears a uniform shirt and has a special name tag. I overheard him telling my dad when they FaceTimed that he arrives fifteen minutes early for each shift. I am really proud of him, knowing Frank, he has already memorized the specifications of each computer.

My mom has had a few meetings or dates on Match.com. One guy was an eye doctor at the mall. He never had kids and was boring. He came over and played Scrabble with us once. He cleared his throat a lot and wore too much cologne. I didn't care for him at all.

Another man brought her flowers and they went out for Indian food. When he dropped her off, I saw them kind of shake hands. Later, he sat in his car for a few minutes looking at his phone with his high beams on. She didn't introduce us, but he walked like an old man.

Now she is sort of dating the one I saw in the picture next to the boat. He is Gary, the veterinarian she had coffee with when I went with my grandma and my brother to see the movie *Chef.* They had one date and then they were both too shy to go out again. I had to help them get to the next level.

Okay, I am *so* in trouble if anyone ever finds this out. I emailed him. She was looking at his picture and his story or bio or whatever it is called, and once again she left the computer on. I quickly wrote, *Please call me, Gary. I want to see you again; it was fun.*

I noticed in one of the pictures of him on his profile that he was sitting on a black pickup truck with shorts and a racing bib with a number on it. He had a golden lab next to him. I told you I always remember colors. Then, one day when my mom came home from work, I told her that a guy with grayish hair and a mustache was driving by in a black truck with a golden lab next to him, and he looked like he was trying to find our house. She asked me why I was telling her this. I told her, "He just looked familiar, maybe like someone we knew from Boulder or maybe someone who knows Grandma."

I added that the adorable golden lab looked right at me, like it was a good luck sign or something.

I swear her face lit up like a Christmas tree. She was picking at her nails, beaming but also looking a bit baffled. I didn't want to jinx it, but it was like I knew he was a nice person. I like that he's a vet and likes dogs.

Gary ended up contacting my mom—she asked him to, wink wink!—and he came over and brought his dogs and we all ate ice cream. We are quiet with each other, but I think he's pretty nice. Gary is about five-foot-ten with a strong build, grayish hair and mustache, and sort of a soul patch or small goatee under his lip. What you notice first are his big brown eyes. He is one of those people who look tired all of the time because they have bags under their eyes. When he sees me, he says, "Hey, Frances, how's it going?" but then goes about his business and doesn't drill me with questions or too much chatter.

My grandma is doing well, but her hip hurts and she limps and seems impatient. She taught me how to paint landscapes, and we paint together on Wednesday nights at her house. She totally gets how I feel annoyed with my mom at times. She encourages me to be mindful, meaning to take a few breaths before I lash out at my mom and then feel guilty about it. I know that I obviously see her more than my dad, but my dad doesn't get under my skin the way she does.

One big accomplishment I had this summer was that

my parents agreed that I was old enough to have a Facebook account, as long as they could monitor it.

Also, I'm officially a middle schooler now. I haven't updated my journal recently. My first day was August 27th. I had a pretty good start at my new school, Branciforte Middle School. My teachers are all pretty cool, and I can go to the library at lunchtime if I want. I have a favorite person at my school. He is the librarian, and his name is Mr. Ziff. His first name is Ollie, which I think is the coolest name I ever heard. It's also a trick you can do on a skateboard. Mr. Ziff told me that he knows Boulder a little bit and thinks it's beautiful. I told him that reading is my passion and that I read *The Catcher in the Rye* when I was in the fifth grade. He has a really welcoming smile and he makes me feel smart. He thought I was an eighth grader, which is what most people think. I have talked to a few people in my classes, but I'm being careful not to say too much too soon. That's what my therapist Joanie once advised me. She told me to be a little bit mysterious.

I'm carrying a notebook to all of my classes, writing down my observations on the teachers and students. It's going to take some time to process everything, figure out what each teacher really wants from me, which books stay in my locker, what I need for each class, etc.

Thirteen

MY MOM AND HER "NEW FRIEND" Gary are obsessed with saving dogs from old people who can't take care of them any longer. He usually visits with two of them at a time. They foster them until they have a home. As much as I love dogs, I have developed a runny nose and itchy eyes. Thanks, Mom. Thanks, Gary.

I feel annoyed by every sound and person around me.

We were working in small groups in math earlier today and some girls were whispering that I was sick and they didn't want to catch the flu from me. I told them it was an allergy, and one girl with too much eyeliner on rolled her dumb cat-like eyes.

I feel snappy, like if I was pushing someone on a swing, I would have pushed them off. They would go *splat!* like a potted plant sitting on a top shelf that suddenly crashes to the ground in pieces, drawing attention.

My mom wants me to meet kids my own age, but frankly nobody strikes me as being interesting so far. I mostly like to talk to Mr. Ziff, the librarian. I noticed he has a lot of Beatles pictures and a lunchbox with their faces, and other things to signify he's a fan. Sometimes during break I try to talk to him, but other kids and teachers constantly interrupt our conversations. I like to tell him about my favorite parts of *The Catcher in the Rye*. I was proud to know that he thinks I'm the youngest person he knows to have read it. I told him I wanted to write a book. He said he'd definitely like to read it. He is probably my favorite person in Santa Cruz. I told him about Frank being on the spectrum, and he said he knows a lot of really wonderful people who have autism. "A few of my aides I've worked with here in the library are on the spectrum," he added. I told him my mom is a therapist, but luckily he didn't ask me about my dad. I don't want anyone to feel sorry for me. I just don't want to bring attention to it, if you know what I mean.

Some kid with a buzz cut kept interrupting our conversation. He kept on asking where the science fiction books were. He was all sweaty at break and tried to sneak his Gatorade into the library. Mr. Ziff told him to finish his drink outside, and the kid wouldn't listen and tried to hide it under his shirt. I wanted to show off my vocabulary, I admit it. "Man, that kid is sure being pugnacious," I said, looking for a reaction.

Mr. Ziff's eyes literally popped out of his head. "That's one of my favorite words! Frances, I'm impressed!" he said.

Mr. Ziff is laid-back, the same way my dad is. I miss my dad. I want him to come visit and take me out of school for a few days. I liked waking up late in the summer. It's hard to fall asleep, and even harder to wake up since school started. I don't appreciate the bell system in middle school. Stupid tardy bells. Give me a break. *Really?* Who has five minutes to leave one class, go to your locker, and then have to be in another class, ready to hear that same awful bell for even another class? *Really?* I wrote this poem after school today. After I ate three pieces of sourdough toast with lots of butter on it. It's for anybody who feels like things are getting under their skin.

Don't Get Under My skin

Don't get under my skin,
If you do, you'll never win
Trying my best to breathe—when people sit on my last nerve
Trying my best to keep my walk straight
Precisely when the sidewalk begins to curve
Personally, I think the tardy bell should never ring
I'd rather hear a drum roll, or a person sing
It's hard to be the mature one—when everyone goofs off
You're the healthy one, and they're the cough
It seems though, germs get the microphone

Sometimes I feel so alone
I want to be eighteen, become my own master
Growing up is slow, I wish it were faster
See me for me, don't look at my age
And this way, we'll stay on the same page
If you get under my skin, I may rage!

Frances Green—September 22nd

Fourteen

I GOT INTO A LITTLE TROUBLE AT school today. I'm not a trained seal. There are too many dumb rules. I despise being told when and where I have to be places. Why can't I be a damn adult already? I'm smarter than most adults. It was a really warm day. My math class ended and I went to the library at break like I usually do. Mr. Ziff was talking to one of the teachers who came in needing his help with something in their class. I became interested in looking at his Beatles memorabilia stuff in his office. I can see some of his things in his office from where we usually talk, but I was increasingly curious. He has pictures of people I assume are his family, and I wanted to look closer. His daughters are pretty. They have his calm, smiling eyes. My next class was PE and I just didn't feel like dressing into gym clothes and being "that new big-boobed brown girl."

I felt like staying in the library, so I did. I noticed Mr. Ziff's desk was sort of messy, and some highlighters were on the carpet. I did what I'm good at: I started organizing. I guess I lost track of time. Break was over, and apparently,one of the girls told the PE teacher that I was in their same math class the previous period. The girl ratted me out, threw me under the bus. Basically, I was MIA. Missing in action.

I was putting paper clips in their correct boxes, sharpening some pencils, and basically wiping down Mr. Ziff's desk with some Clorox wipes I found when I heard my name called on the loudspeaker. *Frances Green, report to the office, Frances Green.* I told myself I'd go in one minute, but I was so pleased by how quickly I was working. The best way to describe it: *I couldn't stop*. Maybe I took it "too far." When I get in the zone, I get super-focused and lose track of time. Probably five or ten minutes after the first announcement, I heard my name called again. It was kind of exciting. Suddenly, Principal Photenhauer walked into the library. She was logging on to one of the computers, and we locked eyes for an awkward quick moment. "Aren't you Frances Green? You just moved here, right?" she asked. I bent over like I was picking up something so she wouldn't think I was walking out of the library office. She had a very friendly face with soft features. She actually said it really nicely, as if she didn't really know. I told her that I was Frances and was on my way to the office. She seemed like she was going to ask me something, and I quickly told her, "I like your turquoise necklace." She thanked me, and that was that. She said, "Let's go to the office, I am on my way there as well." Her cowgirl boots made a comforting but clunky kind of noise. I kept on thinking about how much I liked cleaning up Mr. Ziff's desk. I almost forgot why I walked into the office. The coast was clear for me except for the office lady with a Spanish accent and penciled-in eyebrows, who asked me, "Why didn't you go to your third-period class?"

I whispered, "It's my time of the month." I went on to say that I had to change and was in the bathroom dealing with bad cramps.

She asked me if I told my PE teacher, and I told her that if I had a female teacher, I would have. "You're still unexcused and you'll serve detention during lunch tomorrow." She wrote my name on a list and told me that my parents would be called. She said that third period was almost over and I should just wait on the bench until the bell rings.

"Can I renew my book please?" I asked politely. She nodded and answered the ringing telephone as I walked back into my favorite room. Mr. Ziff was humming and writing something on his calendar.

"How do you like your new desk, Mr. Ziff?" I asked. I could hardly conceal my excitement. My ears felt hot and I imagined I was turning red, but I didn't care.

He looked confused. "Oh my gosh, Frances, so you're

the one who cleaned it?" You did a phenomenal job. When did you do this?"

"During break," I answered. If only he knew.

He high-fived me, and just then the bell rang.

Around dinnertime that night, my mom got an automated message that I wasn't in my third-period class. She was flossing her teeth and casually asked me about it. I told her, "I had a nasty period."

That usually makes people look at you like they feel sorry for you, I mean, when you talk about your period and all.

"Oh, well, then why did your teacher mark you absent, I mean, if you were there?" she asked as she pulled some corn or foreign object out of her mouth. She didn't seem that worried or even like she was waiting for an answer. I told her it's a new school and they have funny rules and that PE teachers should be female for the female students. She was looking in the mirror at her teeth and seemed to forget that the school called her.

I asked her, "What were the girls' bathrooms like when you were in middle school?"

She said, "They were cold and sterile."

I told her they haven't changed. I added this: "I think bathrooms should be colorful. Artistic. They should have a couch and magazines, like a real waiting room."

Frances Green has a plan for talking to parents when you think you might be in trouble. Ask them what it was like for them at their age. Look interested. Sometimes I throw in a compliment, like telling them the shirt they're wearing looks nice, or that other kids have parents who don't really listen, but that you appreciate the fact that you and your family members can talk about anything.

I used to pretend I had headaches at my old school in Boulder. The school nurse had really nice art in her small office. She told me her kids went to the Waldorf School and they did a lot of art. Kids at the Waldorf school don't use the color black. So this nurse had about four big-framed pieces next to a little cot that I would pretend to be asleep on until I got picked up. I liked when my dad would pick me up best because he always played jazz music in the car. It makes me sad that he doesn't know my school or my new house yet. Maybe I'll make a good friend with someone this year who will fly back to Boulder with me and visit my dad and Chloe. We'll all fly back to Santa Cruz together. My dad will stay for a week or two.

I had detention the next day, no big deal, except for the fact that I starved to death. I don't like to eat my lunch inside when it's sunny outside, so I didn't bring my lunch into the sterile room I had detention in. Mr. Ziff thanked me again for cleaning out his desk. He didn't realize that my favor to him bought me detention. It was worth it. Well, sort of. I hate being hungry, and I don't want a reputation as a young lady who gets in trouble.

Mr. Ziff told me that he has homework club before and after school and that he could help me if school was hard. I expected him to ask me about my dad, but he didn't. During lunch, I walked by some kids playing basketball, but I didn't ask to play. I prefer to think that I'm simply gathering information by observing. I'm slowly starting to make some friends in Art and Core, but we just make small talk in class. Once I imagine spending time with these girls after school, I think about doing laps at the gym or reading in my room, and that sounds far more mollifying. So far, other than Abby in my Core class, I don't really want to spend time with my peers.

I got my period early this month, probably because I lied about it. My mom is talking about other therapists she works with, and she seems to be good friends with an older divorced lady named Mary. She comes to the house and they play chess at the kitchen table. Frank walks to his high school with this guy named Mitchell, and they're in the same RSP class. Frank's acne is getting worse. My mom and I tell him not to pick at it, which is ironic because my mom is such a nail picker. It's really habitual. I like that word, *habitual*. Everything is okay, I just feel like I'm trapped in school. I feel the best when I'm swimming or organizing things for people. I don't like math at all, and I look forward to coming home and being in my room. My grandma bought some pretty yellow paint, and we are going to paint my room on Saturday. I think we may even use stencils. I'm getting stoked!

My dad and I FaceTime and text often, and he sends little videos of Chloe eating spaghetti or something like that from her little red chair. He doesn't seem to miss me and doesn't really ask how my new school is. I feel a little lonely, a little bored, a little excited about my new life, and yet a little like I'm-resting-before-I-have-a-big-burst-of-energy kind of feeling.

Fifteen

MY MOTHER HAS A TON OF BOOKS, just like my dad. Before my dad moved out in Boulder, the two of them could have easily opened a bookstore. I am drawn to one book called *The Indigo Children* by Lee Carroll and Jan Tober. My parents told me when I was about six years old that I was an "indigo child." They said I didn't like to be told what to do, I became fixated on organizing and making lists at a young age, and that I fit the criteria for being one. I haven't had time to read the whole book, but I think part of it weirdly does describe me. Just like Frank gets an IEP and special help, I think I should be allowed the freedom to do things my own way.

I mostly miss the warm afternoon rain in Boulder and taking walks in the wildflowers. I don't really miss the people, except my dad and Billy Morgan. I had a therapist named

Michelle when my parents divorced, and she once asked me if I thought I got less attention because Frank has autism and I don't. I really didn't know the answer and still don't. I get enough attention; I just wish that I could pick the classes I want, like in college. I want attention when I want it, and then I want it to go away when I want to be alone. Intuitive attention, I guess I'd call it. I want the world to know that it's hard being a sixth grader in a new school in a brand new state. I wish my school file listed my color as "indigo" instead of "mixed race," because then I'd be allowed to do my own thing and show up for classes when I choose to, *not* when they tell me.

I miss my friend Billy, who lived near me in Boulder. He is two years older than me and always talks about interesting things. We love watching movies together. He's really short and has red hair that is always cut really close to his ears. I call him "Ginger," which he thinks is a funny and very cool name. His dad is a pilot and is away a lot on trips all over the world. When I would go over to his house, his mom put out a laminated sign that read *Shhh! Captain Morgan is sleeping. Don't wake him up!*

Billy wasn't really encouraged to play sports. He plays piano and sings really well. He told me once when we were hiking that some of his cousins and his aunt thought he was gay, and so maybe he was; he wasn't sure. We were eating cucumber and cream cheese sandwiches by Red Rocks. I felt like kissing him, just so that he could feel I was listening to him. My hands felt sweaty and I felt like my toes were rising up, like I was riding on an elevator. Is that weird? I haven't ever kissed anyone. He is average-looking, I suppose. Not super cute, but not unattractive. I like to hang out with him, and we tell each other things we wouldn't tell other people. I never did tell him that I wanted to kiss him. I really didn't want to kiss *him*; I just wanted to kiss somebody. That's my secret. We never talked about him being gay again. Billy and I used to talk about the other kids at our school, as we both disliked the same ones. We both played piano at the talent show, and my performance was right after his.

Billy and I chat on Facebook and text each other. He is probably my best friend in Boulder. Just like everyone thinks I'm fourteen years old or older, everyone thinks he's like twelve years old, which really bugs him. Billy is really a fast runner and told me he runs when he gets stressed.

I like to do laps in the pool while I think about stuff. I think about everything all the time. The counselor at Branciforte Middle School introduced himself to me at the sixth-grade orientation and asked me what I liked to do. I told him, "I like to swim and think." He told me he runs a game club during lunch a few days a week and asked me if I knew how to play chess. I told him I did, and that I play with my brother.

I have to say that even though my mother gets on my nerves, she's a good mom to Frank and me. She gives us room in our room. Billy's parents are really strict, and even though his mom was always nice to me, she always said her dumb rules at their dinner table. She said something like, "Billy, don't clear your plate until Frances is finished with hers." I just don't get it. That puts enormous pressure on kids, and all we're doing is eating. See what I mean?

The first few weeks of school aren't too bad, but I don't like the rules in PE and now we have to set up homework notes for math by keeping these journals, argggggggg…it really bugs me! We have to do these Cornell notes weird thing on our journals, literally setting them up *exactly* like the teacher.

I've been reading through the indigo book last week. Here's a good part that stands out for me:

> They come in with their intentions and gifts easily identifiable from birth. They can suck up knowledge like a sponge, especially if they like or are drawn to a subject, which makes them very advanced in their areas of interest. Experiencing life helps them learn best, so they can create the experiences they need to help them with their current problem or area where they need to grow. They respond best when treated like a respected adult.
>
> —Debra Hegerle, interviewed in *The Indigo Children* by Lee Caroll and Jan Tober

I rest my case. Just treat me like a respected adult.

Sixteen

I DON'T WANT TO SUPPRESS MY creative expression. I want my writer's voice to be *mellifluous*!

The weather is nice here, sunny but not too hot. I keep noticing that the sky seems a lot lower than in Boulder. Last week we went to the boardwalk with my mom, Frank, and his friend Mitchell. It was okay, but my mom talks about Gary too much. We were in line waiting to ride The Cave Train, and, although nobody seemed to be listening, she went on and on, saying, "Gary takes so much time with each animal, especially the sick ones, and he cared for his dying wife until the bitter end."

My mom is a sucker for sad things and depressing movies. Maybe that's why she is a therapist. We are now fostering two cats and two dogs, but all I hear about is how Gary knows everything about what they need. One of the dogs is a Jack Russell mix or something, and my mom constantly holds it and carries it everywhere. One of them barks a lot, which really bugs Frank, and he keeps telling it to "Shut up, please."

Gary comes over on Wednesdays and on the weekends mostly but leaves after dinner. One of his dogs, named Frisbee, is always with him. I take her on walks around the neighborhood. I overheard my mom telling her friend Mary that Gary looked like some actor named Sam Elliot. I googled Sam Elliot, but other than having gray hair, they don't really look anything like each other. I don't understand why hair turns gray. If there is life on other planets, do people age and have gray hair? Oh yeah, I was talking about Gary. Like I said, he often brings over ice cream. He gave my mom a small aquarium that nobody was taking care of at his office. It's super cute and has a castle and pretty blue and purple rocks. We keep it in the living room next to a giant beanbag I like to sit on while I type away or read. We have two angelfish. I named them Leon and Lenny. No particular reason.

Gary is widowed, I think, and has an older daughter who is a food writer in Miami. That's about all I know. He also likes the Rolling Stones and gives Frank a lot of attention for being an expert on them. He brought over some pictures he took at one of their concerts that Frank has been scanning for his archives.

Today we all went to Half Moon Bay to pick out

pumpkins. I took some pictures of all of us posing with our various pumpkins, and a few of Frank and Mitchell high-fiving each other on a haystack. Mitchell doesn't talk much, but he spends a lot of time with Frank, who also doesn't talk much. I was sitting in the back seat of Gary's truck with Frisbee stretched out over my legs, with Frank and Mitchell. Gary was driving and my mom was in the front. We stopped by a little café selling smoothies, and I saw someone selling or fostering kittens. I knew the answer would be "no," but I asked anyway.

I offered, "Let's get a kitten. They obviously need homes."

"There are too many older rescue animals needing homes in Santa Cruz. Nobody needs to buy new ones," Gary said as he took a straw and swirled his smoothie. I noticed he has very large hands. I agreed with his comment, but I hadn't asked him for his opinion. My mom likes him, I can tell. They looked like they would hold hands for a minute, and then they kind of stopped. I pick up on everyone's nervous tension. "How did you meet my mom?" I asked, a little surprised that the question in my head had a voice attached to it. He smiled, his thin lips stretching over a few jagged, yellowish bottom teeth.

"Frances, that is a little personal," my mother interjected as she handed Mitchell a smoothie. Her face was suddenly blotched with a deep raspberry color. I swear she glared at me.

"Raych—it's fine; it's just a question. I got this," Gary

said, as if he was up to bat and somehow knew he'd make a base hit. Why did he call her *Raych*? Her name is Rachel.

I let him talk. I could feel myself breathing slowly, like I had all the time in the world. I sat in one of the café chairs, folding my hands, patiently waiting for the interview question to be answered. Frank and Mitchell were sitting at their own table, oblivious to the three of us.

"So, your mom and I both work. We work a lot," he started. He rubbed his hands together, as if he was warming them to sift sand. "When you get to a certain age, it's hard to meet new friends to do things with, unless you go to bars, which I do not."

"Which I do not either," chimed my mother, sounding like she was on Team Gary.

He continued, "And so modern times have created a social life on websites, and that's how we met. We met for coffee. We both love animals. Does that answer your question?" He looked at me straight in the eye. He didn't look nervous, tense, or like he wanted to end or prolong the conversation. It was a neutral answer.

"So, you're divorced too, Gary?" I asked, as if we knew each other from college.

"I'm actually widowed seven years now. My wife had cancer, uterine cancer. Her name was Melissa."

The café suddenly seemed quiet, although there was techno-beat music coming out of speakers near the wall next to the napkins.

"I'm sorry for your loss," I said, my voice sincere. My mom looked uncomfortable.

"We had to put our family dog down about a year ago. Franny knows about loss," offered my mom.

"Shall we get out of here and drive our new pumpkins home?" suggested Gary, stirring his smoothie once again. "Or Frances, do you have further questions for me?" He chuckled this time and I felt more at ease.

"Why yes, I do," I said, but honestly I didn't have any questions in mind.

"Okay, go," said Gary playfully, as if this was a game show.

"I need a few minutes," I said as we all walked to the truck on the damp ground. I watched my boots crunch a bunch of leaves and pretended there was a shelf of questions I could choose from. We buckled our seats in his truck, listened to Frank and Mitchell burp and laugh, and as soon as we got on the two-lane highway overlooking the ocean, I asked meekly, "Do you plan on getting married again?"

My mother put her face in her hands, shaking her head back and forth.

Gary filled his cheeks with invisible air, exhaling deeply.

I brought a book I was supposed to read for Core with me and decided that I could always open it up and start reading if the silence got too thick.

A fast response came within seconds "I've learned to

live each day as a gift, not expecting anything but staying open to whatever comes my way."

I started reading and just said, "Uh-huh," or something of that nature. He cleared his throat and started talking again.

"To tell you the truth, I enjoyed being married. How about you? What are your plans after you graduate, in what, seven years?" he asked.

"Professional organizer, psychologist, vet, and writer," I replied.

Gary laughed out loud and said, "Hey, how about a pet psychologist and you can write a book about them living in organized kennels?"

We all giggled. I read J.D. Salinger's short stories on the way home. Frank and Mitchell played a pool game on their phones and nobody was talking. I studied Mitchell's face, something I do to everyone when they aren't looking. He kind of has a squished up face and a very flat nose with large nostrils. Whenever my mom offers him something to eat or drink, he answers the same: "I'm good." He doesn't look up much. From the boring back seat of the truck I announced, "I miss Boulder and want to go back for Thanksgiving."

My mom turned around, offering me a piece of gum from a tub she always carries around. She told me that she'll email my dad, and we can discuss it.

"Or…" I began slowly, wanting to see Gary's reaction, "Dad and Ingrid and Chloe can come here."

Gary was looking at the road and drumming his hands softly on the steering wheel, while my mom was staring me down, as she often does. In my head, I said the word *perhaps*, just knowing she would say that in about a nanosecond.

"Perhaps. We will see," said my predictable mother Rachel. Told you I am psychic.

Why does everything take so long? I'll ask my dad if I can come for the holidays or see if he wants to come, and he probably will say that he has to check with Ingrid's work schedule and that maybe he's going with her to Germany, even though he's been saying that for like three years.

I sent him a text with a lot of hearts. I wrote: *Please consider making your daughter Frances very happy by coming out for Thanksgiving. Maybe we can have time just for us.*

He responded about twenty minutes later, while we were still driving: *Sounds fun! Maybe I can come out early and Ingrid and Chloe can visit another time.*

I just flat-out don't like sharing my dad with a new family. It's cool having a little stepsister, but it's complicated, if you want to know the truth. I'm going to swim every time I feel there's too much in my head. I have contract PE now because I swim so much and I told the school counselor I would try out for basketball in early spring. Contract PE means that you don't have to take regular PE classes as long as you document what physical activity you're doing away from school, like yoga or swimming or intensive dance or something. Now, instead of taking PE, I am Mr. Ziff's library aide.

I started feeling restless and claustrophobic in Gary's truck on the ride home. I just wanted to be home in my quiet room, or do hundreds of laps. Maybe it's growing pains, but often I have an uncontrollable urge to stretch my legs out.

When we came home, I knocked on my grandma's door because it was locked. She had been napping but looked happy to see me. We threw our swimsuits in a bag and decided to walk to the gym.

Gary started up his engine and adjusted the mirror. "See ya around, Frances. Glad we got our pumpkins today."

I said, "Goodbye, and thanks for today." I pet Frisbee and rubbed her on top of the head, just the way she likes it. He drove away slowly.

As we walked toward the gym, my grandma took my hand in hers and said, "Well, do we like him?"

I noticed the clouds in the sky and realized I was walking slower than usual.

Like my mom would say, I answered, "We will see."

It seems my grandma doesn't bring up my dad much because she doesn't want me to be sad, but if I ask her if she still likes him, or if she thinks Chloe is pretty or smart, she always says, "Yes." She nods her head as if she's trying to convince me.

My grandma squeezed my hand hard but said nothing.

Seventeen

MR. ZIFF HELPS ME UNDERSTAND THE math I'm learning. My teacher is commendable and explains stuff, but I like the calm voice that Mr. Ziff uses to explain math operations, and he shows me shortcuts. I've always found librarians fascinating, maybe because I've loved books all of my life. Anybody who actually gets paid to work in a library receives my standing ovation. A well-trained librarian can explain anything in the world and I'll gladly listen, even if it is boring, like telling you about the inside of a car engine.

When math is just numbers and symbols, I totally understand. When math has too many words, it freaks me out, and I don't know what I'm supposed to do. I love numbers and predictable systems.

I faked being sick last Tuesday because I felt like

sleeping in, and I also had my period. I was bored as soon as my mom and Frank left the house. I looked around my mom's room to snoop. I couldn't find anything out about Gary. He left no clues or items. The only thing my mom had out was Frank's school file. My mom had written a letter to Frank's case manager, Ms. James, because she wanted the school to know that Frank's dad lives in a different state and she wants to meet the team on a regular basis, with or without him being present. My mom has always reached out to our teachers, I think since Kindergarten, giving off that "let's talk about anything and everything" kind of vibe. I've always read my brother's special education files. I want to understand him more, and I figure that I'll take many college classes on the brain in the future. The paper left out of the file that I found was just a copied email from Frank's Workability special ed teacher, stating that Frank had excellent attendance and is well liked at his job at Best Buy.

I made pancakes and Trader-Joe's-brand Italian sausage and then sliced up some cantaloupe pieces. I was all caught up with homework, so I just read more short stories by J.D. Salinger on the couch. I usually try to do my homework right after school each day to get it over with, and then a few days a week I go swimming. My grandma timed me; I can hold my breath for seventy-five seconds. When I swim, my bored and sad feelings disappear like quicksand.

I took a nap for a little while. My mom called me, and

I reported that my cramps were a nine on the zero-to-ten pain scale, ten being the worst pain of course—but just between us, the real number was about a three.

The next day, after I came back from school and finished my double homework, I went swimming with my grandma. While I was doing laps, I imagined being interviewed on TV. I'd be the featured guest, like on the Ellen DeGeneres show. I'm a humorous writer who lives in Colorado and California. I solve problems for people and also organize their houses. Rich people pay me a lot of money, and there is a long waiting list because I am popular. And super-efficient and effective. If I like my customers and they're poor, I won't charge. I'll also be interviewed for my poetry. I think of things when I swim, hold my breath, and then later I type what I was thinking about. My sixth-grade teachers will say, "I never knew Frances could do all of that. She was introverted and daydreamy, not super quiet, but not an outspoken and confident girl who said she could help everyone."

Giving free swimming lessons will be my charity. I'll make so much money from organizing that I will make sure every kid in my community knows how to swim.

A few weeks ago at the pool, I met a girl who goes to a private school. Her name is Alexandra, and she seems a bit conceited. She has long blonde braids and straight teeth with a retainer. She brags about testing off the charts and claims she was reading books since she was three years old. She closes her eyes when she talks, keeping her hands on her hips as if they're glued. She asks me questions, then interrupts me and talks about herself. If she were a basketball player, she'd be a ball hog. You catch my drift. She also does laps in the pool and kind of stares at me. I was doing some dolphin flips and noticed she'd hung her towel and bag and was waving very excitedly like we were besties. I dove in the water and stayed under as long as I could. It was a good time to practice holding my breath, and I really wasn't in the mood for her shenanigans. She caught up to me and said, "Would you care to race?"

I said, "I'm actually trying to hold my breath to set my personal best record. Maybe next time."

I considered telling her all about hypoxic breathing, but then if she's interested she'll probably want to compete with me, and then I'll be forced to spend time with her.

She crossed her eyes and mumbled something I couldn't really hear. I felt the need to stay away, like she was a big piece of horse poop with flies hovering over.

Last week when I was tested, I was able to hold my breath for seventy seconds, but I'm not sure it was accurate. My mom used a stopwatch and was certain she timed me correctly. No way could I be getting worse! Knowing my mom, she got distracted or didn't start timing me when she said she did. My grandma made me a cup of chai when we got home.

It's my most favorite thing in the world to drink. She asked me about what I wanted to do for Thanksgiving. She kind of seemed clueless, like she didn't really know what she wanted to do. She depends on me for my opinion about things. I think I might study Buddhism when I get older so I can focus on being gentle with everything and everyone and not hurt anyone with words, actions, or even thoughts. My dad was adopted by an older couple in New York and was an only child. They died before he married my mom, so I never knew them. My grandfather Morris on my mom's side was very political, and he retired and moved to Cuba. They divorced when my mom went to college. I only remember him a little bit, and my grandma doesn't bring him up. I saved a few birthday cards from him and a framed picture of a horse he sent me a few years ago, but he pretty much is out of my life. My mom says it's best not to talk about him around my grandma. I guess this is why my grandma is so important to me. She's really my only grandparent. And I'm her only granddaughter.

She tries to be close to Frank but thinks he doesn't really notice her. He's kind of that way with everyone, like I said. I don't always feel noticed at school either, not noticed for the parts of me that I know are exceptional. I want to make friends. It just seems really hard.

I didn't mention Halloween, because it wasn't really a big deal. I dressed like a pirate and answered the door for trick-or-treaters. I miss the snow, making crafts, and basically all of my Boulder memories of Halloween. I was invited to a party from one of the girls in my Core class, but I just didn't feel like going. Candy gives me a headache and makes me thirsty. Thanksgiving is coming up quickly. It should be important to me because it usually is, but I'm afraid to be disappointed. Other kids seem to have a normal family.

"Well, Grandma, what if my dad and Ingrid and Chloe come here for Thanksgiving?" I asked.

She said, "It's up to your mother." She was washing the dishes and talking loudly over the running water. She asked me if I thought Frank would like them to come. I threw my hands up in the air.

"Time for seconds on chai, my little teenager," she announced, walking back into the living room. She used a frother to steam up some milk for the chai and leaned in, almost whispering. She said, "Should Gary be invited if we cook for the family? He seems like a nice guy. I don't know where he lives or if his daughter visits, but it's fine with me if he comes."

I answered, "He brings his golden lab, named Frisbee, everywhere he goes, and I always want to see her, so it's fine with me."

My grandma nodded and said, "Yes, he is okay."

I started to imagine cooking a big meal and making whipped potatoes like I do every Thanksgiving. I sent my mom a text, telling her I wanted to talk to her about an idea. I found an emoji on my phone that looked like holiday food and I made a bunch of exclamation marks and took my wet towel out of my bag. Whenever my grandma dries my clothes in her dryer, they smell better, so I threw it in her dryer. I decided to go home and make quesadillas and salad for dinner.

My mother wasn't in a good mood when I walked into the house. I said hello to her, and she had on these old lady glasses she uses when she needs to read something up close. I asked her if she saw my text, the one about Thanksgiving.

"Dammit, we barely got through October," she said. "Jeez, Fran, how do I replay messages? I can't figure it out on this new phone."

I stood behind her as she was seated at her desk in the living room, and saw again that she tried to cover up a pimple. She made it look really bad with a different almost orange-colored powder. I was just going to tell her or hand her a mirror, but instead I took a deep breath. I went to this Buddhist meeting thing in Boulder with my dad last year, and there was a workshop for kids and teens about holding your breath instead of reacting negatively.

I held my breath for thirty seconds and then showed my poor mother how to replay recent voicemail calls. She took off her glasses and told me to come closer. She gave me a quick and nervous hug. I've been taller than her since

April, my last birthday, so as I looked down over the top of her head, I also noticed she was sprouting a few grey hairs. She made me listen to a call from the school counselor. Not my school counselor, but from Frank's school. Two teachers are concerned that Frank isn't doing group work in math or English. The counselor wants to meet with the family and also his Resource teacher and case manager. My mom played it again. "Is it me, or does this person not seem to understand Frank's issues?" she asked, her eyes twitching. She continued, "Damn, I hope they got his IEP right this time."

My mom has always been overly sensitive about Frank when it comes to school. An IEP is an individualized educational plan. Every kid with a learning disability gets one. My mom always gets worked up each year with new teachers. It's kind of like she wants to bring attention to Frank, but then she doesn't want kids in regular classes to know that he's different. It's complicated.

It wasn't a good time to bring up Thanksgiving, but when I was looking for something to eat at eleven that evening and snuck by the computer area, I saw this email my mom had sent. My mom prints out anything that has to do with Frank and his IEP at school. She keeps files on all of that stuff.

Kevin-

Please contact Frank's school and RSP teacher. You have all the info. I need you to be crystal clear with the IEP team that Frank works best independently. Maybe we can hold the meeting with you on the phone, or on a live video chat. I am counting on you to be his advocate.

Fran is moody, but her grades are good. She wants you and family to come out for Thanksgiving. Kids are on break Nov.23-Nov.28th.

Rachel

I just timed myself typing this email. Three minutes, twenty-four seconds. I'm getting fast. I didn't appreciate being called moody. The hardest part of snooping is that you have to pretend that you don't know what people are saying or writing. It leaves me in a bind, if you know what I mean.

Later that night, my dad called me. He said he has some free miles on Southwest and probably will come out for Thanksgiving. I could hear Chloe singing her ABCs in the background. "Dad," I said, "what about I have an idea…"

We used to do a lot of word games in the car and after dinner. "What about I have an idea" is code for a thinking game, like, *What about I have an idea of naming all vegetables that are green?*

For some reason, it was hard to squeak out what I wanted to say. I was holding my phone very close to my face and felt like I was whispering. I asked him again if he could come by himself. He was talking about something else and didn't hear me. I tried again.

"Dad, remember I asked before? Do you think you could come alone?"

I felt like I sounded like a little girl.

He said, "Umm…I'll think about it. I'll try, okay, Franny?"

That's all I really want to say about my dad right now. I felt disappointed. I just wanted him to say, "Why sure, Frances. Of course, I'll be there."

Everything seems to be moving so fast. It's been a couple of weeks since I had the chance to write things down. I've had a few talks with Joanie. I like to make hot tea in her lobby and sit cross-legged on her comfy couch. I feel like she likes me. She has a really expressive face and I like her laugh. I talk to her about my dad a lot. She probably senses that I'm mad at him, but really I like him, so I kind of pretend I'm not mad enough to make a big deal out of things. She just lets me talk about stuff, and before I know it her chimes ring and it's time to go. I like looking out of the window at all of the people on Pacific Avenue. She did ask me if I've met any kids at school I connect with.

"I met a really nice girl named Abby in my Core class, but we don't hang out outside of class," I answered, watching a bright orange fish dart under a treasure chest.

When I'm in therapy, I either look out of the window or at her aquarium.

"Would you like to do that, I mean, see her outside of class?" she asked me, but I was enjoying the aquarium now and felt quiet and reflective. I could hear the gentle sound of the pump and the fish wheel turning.

"I really don't know," I answered. "I mean, maybe I would."

After a few minutes of watching the fish, I told her that I'd try to reach out to Abby more, and would maybe look for her during lunch. Abby likes to read big novels like me, and she's really artistic. Abby, Joanie, and Mr. Ziff are the only ones I confided in about writing a book about moving to Santa Cruz. Abby was 48 percent interested and Joanie and Mr. Ziff appeared 110 percent thrilled and eager to read what I have so far.

"Did you write when you were a teenager?" I asked while Joanie stood up as the chimes continued to remind me that my time was over.

"Sure did, and I still do. It's a great outlet," she said and took my empty cup of tea.

During dinner that night, I was grating Parmesan cheese in preparation for the minestrone soup, and I realized that I hadn't brought up the weird text I got from Ingrid last week. I wrote down on a sticky a reminder to bring it up with Joanie, but then I forgot. Not sure why it bugged me so much, but it did. I guess I feel a little guilty. Supposedly, my dad told her that I wanted him to come for Thanksgiving alone, and not with her and Chloe. I did *not* know that he told her. So when he told me that he'd try to come out a few days before Thanksgiving, while she'd stay in Boulder with Chloe, I sent her sad faces in a text and told her I was sorry she wasn't coming. Her text to me was this:

Dear Frances,
Your dad informed me that you wanted him to fly out alone, and not see us. I was disappointed but agreed. Why did you tell me then that you were sorry I wasn't coming? It is confusing to me, and Chloe wants to see you. Please, from now on, tell me the truth.
Love,
Ingrid

Awkward, right? My dad said to let it go, not to worry. Things sometimes stay with me for a long time, like a resentful aftertaste. I don't like to have people mad at me, even when I know I'm right.

I can now hold my breath for seventy-four seconds, but it makes me dizzy. Sometimes if I eat too much dinner, I can only hold it for a minute.

Eighteen

THERE IS A SARCASTIC KID AT school nobody really likes. His name is Miles. He has short hair, burps salami, and he interrupts everyone, including the teacher. He is in my Core class, and unfortunately we have silent reading together at the same table. One of my favorite books is called *Are You There God? It's Me, Margaret* by Judy Blume. The book I have is really my mom's copy, and, weirdly enough, she had it when she was a teen. Well, Miles always tries to get kids to laugh, but he's annoying as hell and he gets sent out of the room a lot. He was trying to read over my shoulder during silent reading and mumbled that I was a God freak. I told him that he didn't know what the book was about and to mind his own business. He grabbed my bookmark and made me lose my place, so I grabbed his slimy fingers and pulled them backward. I just wanted to stop him; I don't like how he gets away with stuff. I didn't want to inflict pain, rather make a point. He made a loud noise, and so we both got sent to the principal's office for making a disruption. I didn't do it hard enough to hurt him, but just to send a clear message. The teacher wrote us a referral.

"Nice one, Miles," I said as soon we both were out of the room. I was embarrassed but mostly mad at him and painfully sick of his attitude. "Your breath stinks, *new girl*!" he said as he hit a locker. I stomped on his shoes as hard as I could. He is about three inches shorter than me, and I could tell he was scared. The vice principal walked by and saw that I was walking with a referral in my hand. He is super nice and welcomed me at orientation at the beginning of the school year. When Miles was far away enough not to hear, I started to tell him, "Miles always bugs people when they're trying to read and then he tore my bookmark and—"

But just as I was telling him this, a teacher pushing a cart of laptops needed his attention, and I couldn't finish what I was saying. He told us to wait in the office for him and he'd be right there. As soon as the vice principal walked away, Miles had to be his dumb Miles self and made fun of how the vice principal walks and talks. I shot him the meanest look I could give anyone. We were waiting on the cold, stiff bench in the office. This really kind office lady named Fe asked if we needed something, and I told her that we were told to wait. In Core class we have been studying ancient civilization, and it irked me that I was missing out because of an immature brat, a callow, impudent child.

Again, he mimicked the voice of my vice principal, slowly extending and then dropping his right hand and saying in a high voice, "Hi everyone, I am gay Mr. Arnold," and I swear I just wanted to punch Miles out so he would quit being such a jerk for good. "You know he's probably gay, right?" said this creepy kid.

The next thing, and I swear it was a second later, the office lady Fe told Miles that his mom just dropped off his basketball uniform. Fe said, "Excuse me, Miles is right here," and in that instant, a tired-looking mom dragging a toddler behind her walked through the office to the bench we were sitting at.

"Miles, what now? Why are you here?" asked his mom, looking like he probably bugs everyone at home as well.

He looked embarrassed. I stood up from the bench. "Frances Green," I said in my most adult voice. "I just moved here from Colorado. Your son ripped my bookmark and won't stop bugging me. I was just reading my book, minding my own business. He also says anti-gay things about people who work at this school."

She looked at me up and down, with her blonde highlights and turned-up nose. While chewing gum and kind of rolling her eyes as if she was on my side, she said, "Thanks for telling me, Frances. He's been on this negative trip lately. I will tell his dad. I'm really sorry…"

Miles's little brother was trying to high-five him, and Miles wouldn't look at either one of us. His mom got close to his face and asked him what was up.

"Uh, she left out the part about bending my fingers back and stomping on my new Vans," he said, kind of stuttering and looking like he might cry. Just then, the vice principal walked over and introduced himself to her.

"Would you like to hear what Miles said about you?" I asked. My adrenaline was pumping like techno music. There was definite tension in the air. Oh yeah! It felt like a movie. I had the proof. Too bad I didn't record him saying that. I know a lot of gay people, and they're awesome. I hate intolerant people. This kid is so mean. I was happy to throw him under the bus. I was excused to go back to class, and that was the end of Miles bugging me. My teacher moved his seat closer to her desk, and we continue to avoid each other like the plague, as the saying goes.

Nineteen

MY DAD TOLD ME IN A TEXT THAT he has to attend a conference and that he'd fly out in December instead of Thanksgiving, giving us more time together. He is planning a trip to San Jose State University and also Harbor High School on December 17 and 18. He already talked to my mom about it, and the loose plan is that I'll fly back to Boulder with him and stay for a week. I just don't know what to expect. Somehow when my dad poses things to me, it always feels like he is getting the better deal; he just wraps things in pretty boxes, making things look better than they actually are. He is like a tricky salesman. Gary and his daughter Carina will have Thanksgiving with us. Also Jean, my grandma's good friend, and I think Mitchell is also invited. I feel like a swarm of bees are having a picnic inside my stomach. I don't know Thanksgiving without my dad, but I don't want the outcome to spoil my first Thanksgiving in Santa Cruz. I'm invited to Abby's to have dessert at the Tannery, that art collective place she lives at. My old therapist Michelle told me that if I get anxious about things, I don't have to commit to anything. I'm learning to say, "Maybe."

The whole school runs in something called, the Turkey Trot. It's an annual tradition/fundraiser, and the whole school runs or walks the last day of school before Thanksgiving break. The sixth-grade science teacher named Ms. Peterson-Lindburg; the seventh-grade Core teacher, Ms. Brandon, and Ms. O'Neil, the math teacher, dress like twins, and I heard they run faster than most of the eighth-grade boys. Someone told me that they run every day before school. I hope they wear deodorant. Did I mention I have a very sensitive sense of smell? Well, I do.

While I was running in the trot, which happened right before lunch, I felt super hungry. The bell schedule was changed, so each class was shortened. It seemed odd seeing all of the teachers wearing shirts with the school logo and tennis shoes. Parents were helping out and standing by orange cones, highlighting the running course, and I recognized the music from the old '80s band Queen blaring.

I was ushered to the starting line of sixth-grade girls, and at the sound of "On your mark, get set, *go*!" I mustered up every ounce of power, and though my stomach was grumbling, I passed up pretty much all the girls when I was about two streets down from the school. Once I got into my rhythm of running and noticed the orange cones and saw some parents and staff people I recognized, I felt better. My stride was comfortable and I found I could easily run fast and jog intermittently.

I thought about what a creep Miles is and wondered if mean kids get meaner or nicer after puberty. Puberty is a weird word, as well as a weird phenomenon of growing hair, bleeding, having your voice change, and being able to be parents if you aren't careful. Personally, I think people are at their best when they're like four years old. I saw Miles a few blocks from school and snickering inside; I placed my hands on my hips and charged past him like a Mustang horse. I felt mollified, like he was a symbol of a dumb little thing that I was much faster, stronger, and smarter than, and I'd leave him in the dust, barely remembering his insignificance. I thought about what it would feel like to hug my dad again, and how flying back to Colorado would be. Joanie suggested that I share my sadness that he didn't fly out alone for Thanksgiving, but I don't feel ready to do that. I admitted to her that it's easier to be angrier with my mom than with him. I imagined what my college will look like, and what kind of shoes I'll be wearing when I walk on stage to get my high school diploma. I thought about Billy and what high school is like for him. He was born in September, so he started kindergarten when he was younger than five years old. God, that sounds so young. When I came toward the finish line, well, about 500 feet from it, I decided to run like my pants were on fire. I heard some people yell, "Go, Frances," and it cheered me on. I got a lot of high-fives.

I received my first award at school, coming in at third place in the sixth-grade girls' race. I received a can of cranberry sauce in a Whole Foods bag, and also a carrot cake muffin. It felt really powerful to run. I would have won a big turkey if I came in first place. Maybe next year. "We will see," like Rachel Goldstein says.

Twenty

THE HOLIDAYS CAME QUICKLY. Having alone time with my dad was exactly what I needed. Other than hopefully hanging out with Abby and going to Boulder, nothing was really planned for Christmas break. My grandma celebrates Hanukkah, and the plan was I'd be back before Christmas. Our family has a strange tradition of putting Christmas lights on our large Benjamin ficus plant in the living room every holiday season. Frank and I get one little present a night and light the menorah. Our biggest presents are on the last night. My dad celebrates Christmas, but since Ingrid came along, it's all about her and Chloe, of course.

I'd been so excited to see my dad, and he finally came to fly back with me. The truth is, I was so excited to see him, but I felt like toning down my excitement because I was let down that he didn't come on Thanksgiving. He apologized for not coming out for Thanksgiving but said he'd make it up to me by giving me the window seat on our flight to Denver, and that he'd be Superdad in Boulder.

The other night, I made beeswax candles for my teachers, and my mom got Starbucks cards for them. I handed them out on the last day and gave the best-decorated envelope to Mr. Ziff. We watched *Elf* in my Core class and sat on top of our desks. I got an award for my presentation on ancient civilization. I really like Core class.

Some of the girls are being a little friendlier, but I don't really trust them. Abby has a cold, and we haven't been hanging out as much.

I packed as my mom sat on my bed and picked her nails. She asked me a bunch of questions about Billy. My dad texted that he was about an hour away. His connecting flight was delayed. Suddenly, the moment I was waiting for appeared before my eyes. It didn't seem real. I was weirdly excited and numb. My dad pulled up, I ran to the street to meet him, and we hugged in front of his rental car for at least two minutes. He turned to kiss me on the cheek but I hugged him really hard, knocking off his glasses and kind of throwing him off balance. He accidentally kissed my ear, which was not pleasant. I don't like the sound of anything near my ear. After he excused himself to go to the bathroom, my parents talked in the kitchen for a few minutes as I threw hair stuff in my carry-on duffel bag. I gave him another hug when I walked back into the living room, and we took a bunch of pictures. My mom said she needed a few minutes to go over logistics with him. They were talking *very* quietly, and I couldn't hear even one word, well, only *she*. I noticed my dad's bald spot is getting bigger. He is growing a goatee and looks more tired than what I remembered from the summer. He gave my mom and my grandma a hug and put a big package for Frank against the Benjamin Christmas tree. Frank hugged him but was trying to fix some headphones and seemed like he wanted to go back in his room. My grandma took a selfie of all of us, and then we headed outside to my dad's rental car. It was a black BMW with a sunroof. We listened to jazz as we went through the windy Highway 17. My mom sent me a text. We had been on the road not even ten minutes. Really? Here is the text: *Don't forget to floss. Don't forget to take pictures of the snow. Love you, Franny!*

Of course, she used the snowman emoji and a happy face.

I told my dad what the text said, and he winked. I love when it's just us, and I get attention only from him. He said, "We barely left Santa Cruz and you already get a text. I figured it was from some eighth-grade boy."

I told him it's only Rachel Goldstein, the floss queen. I asked him if she was always so obnoxious about teeth brushing and dental floss. He said that he doesn't really remember.

He looked up at the mirror though and checked his teeth. "I think she did make a big deal out of teeth, now that you mention it."

We were quiet for a while. He was looking at the road. It started to rain.

"What's up, baby? You're being quiet." He reached for my hand.

"Just tired," I replied. I was waiting five months or so for this time with him and just didn't know what to talk about, you know, how to bring up anything.

He touched my hair for a second, perhaps nervously, and then, adjusting the heater in the car, he added softly, "Yeah, me too. We're gonna have a spectacular time, though. Just chill for now; go to sleep. I think this seat reclines all the way." He looked for levers under my seat with his right hand and started to swerve a little.

I reminded him, "I still get car sick sometimes; I don't want to put my seat down. I'm cool." I tried to say it in a voice that would sound appreciative, but I just wanted him to make me feel better about stuff without reminding him.

We shared some trail mix and arrived at the car rental place near the airport. Only when we took our seats on the plane did it start to feel normal.

We played tic-tac-toe, drew pictures together, and I told him a lot about my classes and stuff. The expression on his face got really bright and happy when I told him I was writing a lot. "Can I read what you have so far?" he asked, "Pa-leeze! Cuz I don't know the teenage mind anymore. I'm an old man now, ya know?" He said this while making his eyes really buggy and twisting his face so he looked kind of crazy. We both laughed.

"Seriously though, Fran. I help a lot of interns and colleagues with writing; I'd love to take a look."

I told him the truth. "It's not a diary, but I write about feelings, personal stuff. My observations on life. Not now, maybe later."

The flight attendant brought us apple juice and little pretzel sticks. They didn't taste very good together. My dad gave me a funny look. He leaned in close and asked, "Do you talk about me in your writing? Just tell me, am I a good guy, or a mean guy?" He sort of laughed, but he reminded me of a kid asking his teacher if he was going to get a good grade on a project or something.

I thought of a good comeback. "Grandma Harriet and Mom always say, 'We will see.' So, we will see." We held hands until our flight landed in Denver.

He said, "I love you, Frances."

And I said, "Love you too, Daddy."

Twenty-One

MY DAD AND INGRID SENT FRANK some computer things and a blue sweater. It arrived sometime while I was visiting Boulder, and every day my mom has been nagging him to send a thank you note. Frank said he texted *thank you* but unfortunately, it wasn't enough for Rachel.

I am back to calling my mom Rachel. I love my mom, of course, but after spending almost a week with my dad, I feel closer to him. I wouldn't want my mom to know this. The cool thing about writing is you can express yourself and not hold back. I just have to be very careful not to leave my laptop around for anyone to read. I am super-duper careful. My mom would be devastated if she knew everything I felt. Joanie always says that big feelings, especially dark ones, have to get out and be released.

I've been thinking more and more about my trip to Boulder. I'm still processing everything. More than anything, it went really fast. I hung out twice with Billy and had dinner at their house. His mom asked me a bunch of questions about my life in Santa Cruz. Billy seemed kind of distant. He was on his phone a lot. He had this big science project he was working on. I kind of felt like an outcast when I was at their house. I slept next to the Christmas tree on a comfortable couch at my dad's. It was a classic Douglas fir with an angel holding a harp on top that almost reached the top of the ceiling. My mom packed Tylenol PM for me because I'm very prone to insomnia. One night I'm certain I just stared at the twinkling lights on their tree all night long, not getting one wink of sleep. There were gifts for me under the tree I pretended not to notice; I didn't want them to know I was looking. Frances is always looking. Okay, I did unwrap the box that the Uggs were in because I was curious. The biggest problem with snooping is that you have to be a good actor and act really surprised, even when nothing is a surprise.

Chloe and I made a fort out of blankets. She is kind of spoiled, but we got along. She likes when I swing her by her feet. I think she looks more like Ingrid than my dad. Her skin is so super light, she could actually pass as Mexican or Brazilian or something. Ingrid and I also got along pretty well. Neither of us brought up the weird text she sent to me about being confused whether or not I wanted her to come for Thanksgiving. Joanie says sometimes it's best to just let things go.

Some of her friends came over to get her one of the nights I was there, and so I got to hang out with just my dad and Chloe. We played chess when Chloe went to sleep. I took his queen with my horse and he pretended to cry. It was pretty funny. I probably could've had him in checkmate, but we decided to not finish the game and instead make some bruschetta, like old times. Afterward we watched a movie. We saw *Mrs. Doubtfire*. I've seen this movie like five times.

I know that Robin Williams committed suicide a couple of summers ago. My whole family was really sad. I can't think of anything worse. I think about his kids and wife. I asked my dad why people would end their lives. He said something like he didn't know, but we need more intervention groups and that Robin was super talented and what a terrible shame it was. He said he lost a friend a few years ago and that he's still in shock that it happened. He said it was a friend who used to start group homes for troubled teens. I kind of remember him coming to the house when I was about six or seven years old. He had a puppy or two with him and he played the guitar. His name was Charles, and he was a really funny Italian man with a thick Brooklyn accent. He was a wheeler-dealer guy who bought things from yard sales and thrift stores and fixed them up and resold them. Anyway, my dad got news that Charles was found on railroad tracks in a little town near New York. My dad shook his head, like he was still kind of in shock when he was telling me this story. He said that nobody could make him laugh the way Charles did. He looked at me kind of funny and said, "Franny, don't ever give up!" He kind of pretended to choke me and then just hugged me and pounded lightly on my back like it was a drum.

I said, "Hell no, Daddy."

I like this memory. I like snapshots in my head like this, when it's only us, nobody else. We watched the movie together, laughing at the same places. I thought about Robin Williams's character, how he dressed up like an old nanny woman just to be with his kids. Would my dad do that? That was probably my best memory of going home for Christmas break, well, I mean, home to Boulder. Just hanging out with him and watching old movies. The part that felt funny, though, was that my dad seemed so comfortable, it was *his* house, and although I'm his daughter, it's his bathroom, his shower, his couch I slept on; all of those things are his world and not mine. They're also Chloe's and Ingrid's things.

Abby told me to write everything I did on my trip in my journal and asked me if I thought it would be weird to go back. Flying back to San Jose, California, made me feel grown up. I enjoyed being by myself. I took my laptop with me and actually read back *everything* I wrote since moving last July, starting with the long car drive. It was like watching a movie about my whole life. I didn't talk to anybody on the plane. A flight attendant escorted me from the gate to the plane. I pretended to be a famous writer. I ate peanuts and drank hot tea with gross powdered cream as I read from the very beginning to now. Before I knew it, we landed, and another nice flight attendant with a bald head and a fancy silver bracelet walked me to baggage claim.

My mom and Gary were standing there waving to me. My ears had not popped, so I felt kind of out of it. The ride home was quiet. I forgot how windy Highway 17 was. I sat in the back of Gary's truck with Frisbee licking my hand and wagging her tail. Some jazzy Christmas music was on the radio, or maybe from Gary's phone. My mom started to ask me questions, you know, like, "So, Frances, tell me. How big is Chloe now? Did you see Billy?"

I told her that my ears needed to pop and I'd tell her in the morning. She got quiet. I probably hurt her feelings. Gary took my suitcase out of the trunk and put it in my room. "Good to have you back, kiddo," was all he said. He smiled.

Abby was texting me, but I was really tired and decided to take a hot shower and go to bed. So anyway, for Christmas I got Ugg boots, two Nina Simone music books, a really cool Bluetooth wireless speaker, and lots of iTunes cards. I will try to learn a few Nina Simone songs. I have piano lessons every Saturday from a nice quiet man named Dean, and I think I'm getting a little better. My dad listens to Nina Simone a lot, even though she died a long time ago.

I got behind in my writing because I joined the school's girls' basketball team and we practice a lot. I hang out with Abby still, and new friends named Linnea and Avona. I became point guard of the team. I have tried to schedule time to write, but it just hasn't been working. Sometimes I start to write, and I daydream and realize that I've been people watching and an hour or two have passed.

I left out Thanksgiving. Like Halloween, there was just not a lot going on to report. It went mostly okay. I had a bad cold for most of the time. Gary came with his daughter Carina, who is a food writer and does marketing for a big cruise line in Miami. She looks like Gary and made really good Brussels sprouts and macaroni and cheese. Frank liked the macaroni and cheese a lot. Mitchell had Thanksgiving with us, and one of my grandma's friends came, who is a retired teacher from Branciforte Middle School. She taught there for many decades. She is my favorite of my grandma's friends. Her name is Jean Calvert and she travels all over the world. We hit it off right away, and she knows many of my teachers. We have plans to go out for Mexican food, just the two of us. She doesn't drive, so we will take the bus or have my mom or grandma drive us. She said when I am in the eighth grade, I'll be published in the book the eighth-grade teacher Wendy Thompson helps out with. Jean might be my writing assistant.

Wendy came to my Core class and talked about this writing program called the Young Writers Program. It's for students who love to write, and we get to publish a book at the end of the year. I'm on the waiting list for April. The class is held at a really cool museum downtown. Wendy dresses in really bright colors and has really pretty hair with straight bangs. She always says hello to me and she invited me to the lunchtime book club.

I mentioned Thanksgiving went okay, but if you peeled the layers of my true feelings, I was super disappointed. I wanted my dad to myself, but even if he had come out for a visit, probably Ingrid and Chloe would've come; so therefore, I wouldn't have had it my way. I tried to make plans with Frank, who pretty much mopes around his room when he's not at Best Buy, but we didn't really do anything except go on a few dog walks and play chess. We both forfeited without either of us getting checkmated, but he's a much better chess player.

There is tension between my mom and grandma. My mom unconsciously tries to get her mother to think good things about her boyfriend. My grandmother is the kind of strong woman who makes up her own mind when *she* decides to. If she was a fish, she wouldn't go for my mother's obvious bait. Gary brings Frisbee everywhere he goes, which gives him automatic points in my book. He put a piece of turkey on Frisbee's nose and said, "Leave it," and she can do that for almost a minute. Gary is a kind man, and he doesn't talk too much, which is something I like, yet I still hear his footsteps in my house. I think that may be a metaphor I just made up. I kind of like how it sounds. Anyway, it just felt odd having him there at the dinner table and not my dad. We FaceTimed on Thanksgiving, my dad and I, but sometimes when I see myself on a screen I freeze up a little, even though the world knows Frances ain't shy! I feel like my braces make me talk funny, not in real life, but when I'm on video chats and FaceTime.

Did I mention that my mom seemed all bent out of shape and emo during Thanksgiving dinner? She dressed up really nice and let me put her hair up, but she's going through something. She is rapidly getting more gray hair.

My hunch is that she's worried about Frank. When she and my dad talk on the phone, she's usually doing the dishes or paying bills online at the same time, and always has my dad on speakerphone. I listened in on a talk they had the day after Thanksgiving. It was Black Friday, and Frank had been working at Best Buy since early in the morning. I heard my mom say, "I met with Frank's teachers and RSP case manager. His grades are pretty bad."

My dad answered, "Just let him be. I know you're a good mom. Let him feel okay about where he is in his life. His job is going well, and he'll graduate; that's the important piece."

My mom said what she's been saying for years and years, "Frank needs structure."

It's kind of ironic though, two people from different races and mindsets raising a teenager. The parent who knows a lot about autism doesn't live with the teenager. There's nothing stranger than people. Nothing.

Twenty-Two

LIFE IS PRETTY CHILL (MY NEW California word), but it still surprises me that the weather and nature's colors don't change much. I've been enjoying wearing a beanie over my wild hair and riding my bike with Abby to West Cliff, where we people watch. It's the most special thing I do with Abby: people watching while we ride bikes. We make up stories with our wild ideas about who these people really are and what their lives are like. I can be 100 percent myself around Abby, but the minute another person comes into our circle, it's like a psychic slam right to the vortex. Everything becomes slow motion and dramatic, and sometimes she can't even hear what I'm saying. Abby even has a fake laugh in front of some of her friends. I'm not trying to sound demanding or bossy, but I really only like to hang out with Abby when it's just us. I told her that once, but she didn't respond. She was in a bad mood and said that she wanted salty potato chips with vinegar because everything seemed salty and sad. I said, "Abs, did you even hear what I said? Is that weird, that I just want us to hang out without other people?"

She just put her hand on her abdomen and said something about hating cramps and she was sick of everything being serious. I don't mean to come off as obsessive, but it's hard to share a best friend, especially when that best friend changes right before your eyes when new people come into the picture. If only we could spend our entire friendship people watching and trying to make each other laugh about our story inventions! I wish this because that's when Abby seems to like me the most. Once I saw a man taking pictures of the fancy houses near the ocean, and I said his name was Sherman and he is a billionaire from London. He pretends to be a real estate agent, but actually he buys houses for himself and is superstitious about sleeping in the same bed, so he actually sleeps all over the world in his many houses. She liked this story a lot. I never brought up not wanting to hang out with her if other people are around, and she didn't either. We get along better since I keep more to myself.

Abby lives with her mom and siblings in an artist's community near Costco. Sometimes I go to sleepovers at her house. I like Abby's mom. Abby has good common sense and isn't afraid to eat the last cookie. She is really the salt of the Earth and gets along with everyone. When I'm bored, I look at all of the pictures I have captured from my camera roll on my phone, and either keep or delete them. It's a passing-time kind of game. Keep or toss, and I get to decide. When I write, it's the same concept. I just have to be very careful not to leave my laptop around for anyone to read, or I guess I can give everyone a code word so nobody would really know.

I joined ASB to learn more leadership (Associated Student Body) and I'm in charge of doing things for my school. I like it. Mr. Arnold told me that he counts on me for my maturity and wasn't happy when he saw I had another referral.

I got in trouble again right after winter break because I told the student teacher in math that she needed to take control of the class. She thought it was rude, and that's why I got a referral. My vice principal told me I was possibly right, but it was a student teacher, and I should just give my math teacher the feedback, period. I understand, but if someone wants to be a teacher, shouldn't they know that they're being ignored? I love talking to Mr. Arnold in his office. He and his partner and their sons go to Mexico in the summer and he has cool Mexican art all over his office. He treats me like Mr. Ziff treats me, like I'm not just a meek sixth grader. He said that since I joined ASB, I'll automatically learn to honor the school rules more. I asked him if Miles apologized to him. I thought he'd tell me, but he smiled and just said, "Oh Frances, you're going to do something amazing with your life, I just know it! Sorry, it's between Miles, his family, and me. Don't worry. Thank you for caring," he added and gave me a fist bump. I like him so much. His teeth are really white. He kind of smiles the way dental hygienists smile, like they know you have to be looking at their teeth. Did I mention I dream about my teeth like all of the time? Mostly they are falling out, or crumbling, and sometimes I'm in a strange bathroom looking for paper clips and glue or something to hold them into place. I wonder what this all means.

Twenty-Three

I HAD A REALLY AWKWARD THING happen over winter break that I failed to mention. It happened the week after I came home from Boulder during winter break. I spent the night at Abby's, who as you know, is my new best friend. Her mom is a live model for art students to draw, and she also loves to sketch in her free time. We decided to get up early and go to West Cliff and sketch, followed by going out to breakfast. We woke up early, and I remembered that I had a new box of art supplies on my desk. Well, I didn't knock on the door when we stopped by my house to get my colored pencils. I just walked toward my room and my mom's door was open. She and Gary were asleep. I was more embarrassed than they were. She kind of leaped out of bed, startled, and said, "Frances?"

I quickly shut her bedroom door and I'm sure I turned

every shade of red. I flipped on my light in my room and looked for the colored pencils. My heart was beating really fast. She put her big sea-green robe on and said quietly, "I didn't know you were coming home so early. I am…sorry."

"You didn't do anything, Mom, it's okay. Where is Frank?" I asked, trying not to look to see if she had pajamas on under her robe. Her hair was messy and she was wearing her reading glasses. "He's at Mitchell's, honey. That's why, oh never mind," she said, tucking her hair behind her ears nervously. She gave me a quick kiss on the forehead, and I quickly left. When I jumped back in Abby's mom's car, I pinched Abby and retold the story. I guess my mom has sleepovers too…

Abby and I are taking a fun class after school on Wednesday, which is our half-day at school. It is called Cartoon Animation. The teacher is named Elijah, and he's my principal's nephew. We sort of look a lot alike. He is also mixed, biracial, whatever you want to call it. Anyway, we learn how to sketch, how to create depth and shadows, how to draw cartoons and stuff like that. I was taking some pictures after school with my phone, waiting for Abby and the rest of the class in the Innovation Center, which is located at the back of my school, where the class is held. One of the eighth-grade teachers saw me standing there, so they let me in. The eighth graders get to work on a book that gets published at the end of the year, so there's a lot of activity with groups of kids and writing tutors coming and going.

That friend of my grandma's I mentioned earlier, Jean, is in China now, but she is going to work with my group in April, I was told. I wish I was in eighth grade so that I could be printed in another book anthology. Anyway, it was going to rain, and I had a few minutes before the rest of my class got there. I practiced taking pictures on my phone with a new app that lets me edit photos. I was standing really close to some framed paintings that students had made. I'd snapped a few pictures when I heard people talking in one of the back rooms. There were two men, about twenty years old or so. One of the guys had a shaved head. They were crouching down, moving numbers on a padlock. They didn't see me. I don't know why, but I took their picture. My heart was pounding. Again, I don't know why. Just then, Elijah came in whistling and opened the main door. The guys walked out, shutting the door behind them. I got distracted by Elijah's high tops and asked where he got them.

Class started, and I started taking notes about cartooning and animation. Abby and I were tasked to put our pictures together and create an iMovie. After class, we walked past the library, and I remembered it was Mr. Ziff's birthday. I gave him a bar of chocolate I had in my backpack that my Grandma bought me and wished him a happy birthday. He was ready to leave on his bike. He thanked me and asked me how I remembered. "Your birthday is on the ninth of January and Frisbee's is on the eighth," I said.

"Who is Frisbee?!" he asked, smiling, meanwhile unlocking his bike and putting on his helmet.

"Frisbee is my mom's boyfriend's dog," I said.

"Frisbee, what a cool name," he said again. He added, "I'll share the chocolate with my wife after dinner." I don't know why exactly, but I felt a twinge of envy. I wish I had someone special in my life who'd share chocolate with me.

Twenty-Four

MY MOM AND GRANDMA HAVE BOTH told me that ever since I joined ASB, I'm a happier person. We brought handmade cards to a local assisted living place for senior citizens last week. We share our ideas at our Monday ASB meetings. I think I mentioned that Gary helps out with fostering animals when older people can't take care of them any longer. One idea I had is taking pictures and making adoption placement cards for the animals. I can put them in the office and post them on our school website, that way anybody involved with our school who wants a dog or cat can go through the adoption process easily.

Mr. Ziff has a picture of Roscoe on his desk, his dog that passed away. I wanted to do something nice for him because he always asks me how my book is coming along and he helps me with my math. One day after school, Abby and

I took our bikes to the local SPCA.

We were both really hungry, so we first stopped off at the corner gas station and pooled our money together. Luckily, we had $5. We bought Starburst, sunflower seeds, Pringles, and water. We ate a little bit, and then washed our hands and walked into the SPCA. I met the most adorable terrier mix named Selma. The lady who worked there let us walk her around the block after I said that Gary Bettano was my mom's boyfriend and we foster dogs. Selma is about three years old and is house-trained and gets along with other dogs. That's what her description states above her kennel. Her owner had to go into assisted living, and nobody could care for her. I called Gary at work and told him I needed to see him ASAP. The receptionist told me he was in surgery but could call me back in about an hour. This wouldn't do. I needed to take Selma home before someone else did. Abby told me, "You don't need to bring more animals to your house. Come on, let's ride home."

I told her that I was incorrigible when it's the right thing, and that's how I operate.

She said, "You're what?"

"Never mind. I'm stubborn on steroids is all," I said as I began texting my mom. She usually leaves The Parent's Center about 4:00 p.m. on Fridays.

COME TO THE SPCA ON 7TH AVE. RIGHT NOW, GARY FOUND A DOG THAT NEEDS A HOME.

I put it in all caps so that she would take it seriously.

Abby and I were sitting on our bikes eating more Pringles when my mom pulled up. My mom got out of the car to make room for our backpacks and took some of our Pringles. "All right, missy, what's the rush?" she asked. Ever since I've been hanging out with Abby, she's nicer to me when we spend time together. She met Abby's mom a few times, and they really hit it off, too.

"Mr. Ziff needs this dog, Mom, and she's perfect," I said, tugging at her arm. We walked my mom over to Selma's kennel, and I could tell she liked her right away too. Selma walked over to her and started wagging her tail. She licked my mom's finger through the cage, and Abby said, "How sad her owner was too old to keep her."

I winked at Abby. The timing was perfect.

"Well, Mr. Ziff will need to do the paperwork and be screened and all that."

I knew she would say that. "Mom, it's a surprise from his wife, so she can't come over here. Gary said one of his patients has been searching for this breed. They know him here, you know. He even called me when I texted him about her. Even look, see he called." I showed her my phone so she could see his number from when I called him. She seemed pleased that I was corresponding with him.

"Frances, it's Friday, there's traffic, and I'm tired. Let's go home. Don't get involved with other people's business," she said as she was holding Selma, rubbing her fingers back and forth over her little ears.

A lady whose name tag read *Tara, Volunteer* intervened. "Ma'am, this dog is going to go fast. She's current on shots, she's very well mannered, and she's been spayed. She'll be gone if you wait until the end of the weekend, maybe as early as tomorrow. She's a keeper. If you have a home for her, I'd suggest you move on this one. Just sayin'." Tara was convincing, because my mom bit her lip and started to look at her phone, I think to call Gary.

"He's in surgery," I said, "but he thinks it's a great idea, and like I said, if for some reason the Ziffs can't take Selma, Gary has a perfect home."

The odds were on my side, like a good math problem. My mom is a sucker for dogs and sad stories. It was Friday, she was tired and didn't want to argue with me, I was with Abby, we had crates at home, and she always said that Mr. Ziff sounds like a mensch (a Yiddish word for a good person).

About forty-five minutes later, following some paperwork and I think $40 or something, Selma sat on my mom's lap as we threw our bikes on the bike rack.

I had to cover my bases. I sent Gary a text:

Gary, we found a perfect dog that my mom really likes, but it's for the librarian at my school. It's best if you don't mention the dog. We're going to foster her until Sunday. She's in love with her. Thanks—Frances

The outcome of this whole dog story is confusing to explain. I procrastinate bringing up the thorny cactus parts. Sometimes I just want to daydream, pretend my life is a movie, and watch passively with hot buttery popcorn. I'm once again in trouble for going *too far*. I don't really feel like talking about it, but instead of letting it overwhelm me, I'll attempt to jot down the series of awful events.

First off, the rat terrier dog at our house scared her away, and the cat doesn't like her either.

Second of all, when I called Mr. Ziff to get his address, (I found his number doing detective work) he sounded very surprised to hear from me. He said he was away in Berkeley at a Cal game and wouldn't be home until Sunday afternoon. When he asked why I was calling, I just said that I needed to drop something by; it was a gift from my parents.

Next, Gary came by the house and checked out Selma. He said she was healthy, but he and my mom were whispering to each other, and the bottom line was this—the dog needs to be gone by Sunday, and my mother said, "Furthermore, Frances, there's something fishy going on."

I searched her face for even a little patch of kindness, and it was clearly not there. Her face had steam coming off of it, like an old, tired industrial dishwasher at a busy restaurant. My body felt tense, scared, riddled with worry, and then my mother, who reads all of these "codependent no more" books had more to say.

"Why isn't Mr. Ziff's wife coming over to get her? I don't have an extra $50, and I expect to be reimbursed. You took advantage of me being tired on Friday, putting pressure on me in front of Abby."

She was kind of shaking her finger at me when she said this. Gary was quiet, avoiding my eyes. When my mom gets mad, or we get into it with each other, he usually goes to his truck, grabs Frisbee's leash, and they disappear for an hour. He stayed for this one, making me feel like I upset two for the price of one.

The big pot of crap soup continued to get stirred. Abby got invited to a roller skating party that I wasn't invited to on Sunday afternoon, and she said in a text that she couldn't go with me to the Ziff's house. Great, I got to look weird all by myself, showing up with a dog they haven't seen and maybe or probably don't want. I just wanted to help.

I called my dad, who loves stories and problems, always trying to side with being fair. He was giving Chloe a bath while Ingrid was at the gym working, but he said he'd call me back. He kind of laughed. "Girl, what did you do now?" he asked. We agreed that he would call back in fifteen minutes. I read over some of my journal while I waited. When are things gonna get good? The thing is, I like Mr. Ziff and I just hoped he'd take the dog and thank me profusely. I like the word *profusely*. It's such a fiery word. I prayed. I have one of those plastic tea lights with a small battery inside and I turned it on and sat in my dark closet. *Please let this work out.* I visualized the whole scenario, like a commercial for shampoo or soap or a Hallmark card. I was thinking of the book *Are You There God? It's Me, Margaret,* and I changed the wording to *Are You There God? It's Me, Frances.* "Please, Jewish or African-American God, or Buddha or whatever you are, please, please, please, let the Ziff family take this dog and I won't make up stories any longer. Well, I'll try not to," I said out loud. It was Sunday. Isn't Sunday like a God or good luck day? I sure hoped so.

My mom and Gary were going to see a movie and grab something to eat afterward, and I asked Gary if I could walk Frisbee while they were out. Usually, they take her everywhere, except for movies and restaurants. He handed me a leash, and Frisbee immediately started to wag her tail and walked toward the door. Sometimes I get good thinking energy when I walk, so I took Frisbee and Selma and a little dog food in a Ziploc baggie and headed toward Frederick Park so I could waste time and then find the Ziff house.

While at the park, I ran into the eighth-grade teachers Ms. Goldfarb and Wendy Thompson, also walking a dog. They know me through ASB They said, "Your dogs are adorable!" I told them that Selma was healthy and needed a home, and that I wanted to surprise Mr. Ziff with her. They looked at each other in a puzzled way. Ms. Goldfarb said, "Mr. Ziff had a dog named Roscoe for many years. They came here to play a lot. I dunno, she's awfully cute, but sometimes people don't get new dogs, but then again, sometimes they do," she said.

She asked Wendy what she thought. Wendy asked if I had told Mr. Ziff anything. "Just that I had a gift from my parents I was dropping by," I said, suddenly feeling shy.

They offered to walk to his house with me. They asked me about my classes, basketball, and stuff like that. It felt safer walking with them. After we walked a few minutes, I was untangling leashes just in time to notice Mr. Ziff's Volvo with the University of California in Berkeley sticker sitting in his driveway. He was standing there, taking something out of the trunk. His front door was open. He looked surprised to see us, but like always, he smiled. He asked Wendy if she was able to download the answers to some social studies test, or something like that. Wendy smiled. "No shop talk on Sunday, Ollie—I mean Mr. Ziff. You know Frances, right?"

I guess I felt out of place and wasn't sure if I should be at his house.

"Frances and I are good library friends; of course I know Frances!" Mr. Ziff met both dogs, and then the rest of this very short visit is foggy. Wendy and Ms. Goldfarb whispered something to each other and excused themselves and walked away. Mr. Ziff seemed like he was in the middle of something and was literally unpacking his trunk. Maybe he remembered that I had something for him. My face got hot, and I wanted to disappear right into the cement. Frisbee suddenly went poop, right by Mr. Ziff's rock garden, and I felt like a big nuisance. Like someone ringing the doorbell with food while a family is inside eating dinner. I had to break the awful silence.

"My mom and her boyfriend have these dogs that they rescue and foster. I thought you and your wife could use one since your dog died. She's free. My mom's boyfriend is a vet, Gary Buttano. So, she's yours if you want her." I could tell my voice was shaking and I was stuttering. He looked confused. His wife came outside while we were talking. We shook hands, and she pet the dogs, but she needed his hand with the hose in the backyard or something. I felt like such a dummy. I felt hatred for myself; my throat was filled with broken glass. They didn't want a dog. I'd have to try to find her a home and talk to ASB about making flyers at tomorrow's meeting. Meanwhile, I lied to my mom, and our current dog and cat are freaking out and don't accept a new dog in the house. Great. Now what? I threw away Frisbee's stinking poop bag in their garbage can and walked away.

"Frances, thank you for coming over and thinking of us. I, I don't think we're in the market for a dog right now, but thank you," he said as the leashes were once again getting caught under my leg.

I walked away, feeling like a dumb kid and not looking forward to the long walk home. I walked home, no doubt with my head down, watched *Modern Family* with Frank, and cried the second my mom and Gary walked inside the house. I don't know why, but I grabbed onto Gary's flannel shirt and sobbed. I had never really hugged him before. I felt lost. Lost and stupid. I was aware that I was making baby sounds. I couldn't help it.

Twenty-Five

ONE DAY I'LL LOOK BACK ON MY middle school experiences. Will I laugh? Will I cry?

I'll be thirty years old. I'll be successful and will go on book signing tours. I'll be the most organized vet or the most helpful psychologist around. I'll smell chocolate milk and pepperoni pizza, and a million memories will start coming up and popping wildly for me, like popcorn at the movie theatre. I'll always remember everything about our school Valentine's dance. I just know it.

The gym was swarming with pink and red hearts. There were a dozen or so balloons, but people were popping them on purpose and screaming, laughing, and stomping on them when teachers weren't looking. I was supposed to sleep over at Abby's, but she's been hanging out with some girls that give me stink eye. This girl named Lakeesha "supposedly" said that I stuff my bra. *I stuff my bra.* Give me a break. Even a bigger lie, I flirt with some seventh-grade boy that she likes in PE. Abby is kind of wimpy. I mean, she's one of my best friends and all, but she doesn't stand up to Lakeesha and tell her how wrong she is. I had to pull this info from her, so imagine all the crapola that people say or think about me that she doesn't tell me. Abby just gets quiet when she doesn't know what to say. I've seen this in action. I don't like Jordan, this seventh grader; I mean, I like him only as a friend. I just play basketball with him. Sometimes I wish Abby wouldn't tell me what people say behind my back. I have to pretend that I don't know, which makes me feel like I'm dumb, which I'm not. My grandma tells me all the time that people will disappoint me and that the secret to happiness is simply knowing who you really are.

So back to the dance...The DJ was really cute and funny too. He had a shaved head and a goatee. He was probably about twenty-two years old, or somewhere in that range. I requested "Boom Boom Pow" by the Black Eyed Peas and he played it. I danced my butt off, but I had a headache. Sometimes cheap cologne goes up my nose, causing me to feel nauseated.

We all danced and threw balloons back and forth to each other. Abby was standing with Lakeesha and Sonia and a couple of other people, but they were just taking selfies and being boring. A really nice sixth grader named Kylie was acting hyper, and we danced like crazy with each other. We worked up a sweat and got everyone to do two separate trains. I've seen her around campus, and I liked the fact that neither of us do stupid middle school small talk. We just danced like nobody was watching, like the saying goes. Kylie has long blonde hair and wears dresses with high tops. Love her style. Her mom was born in Japan, but she's blonde too. That's all I really know about her. The best part of dancing is that you go into the moment. My heart was racing as I kept smacking the pink and red balloons that were tossed to me.

I was sweating like crazy and my neck felt like someone was twisting it. Everything seemed so big and loud and in my face. I walked outside, taking a few sips of fresh air like it was water. The sky was cloudy, and nobody saw me except for a science teacher I had seen on campus before; he was locking his door. It felt better being outside. Sometimes you just have to listen to your body.

I walked back inside the gym and hung out with a couple of teachers selling pizza and water. I hate and like school dances. I get lost in the loud music. I like how everyone dances together, and I love making a train. I don't like dances because I feel awkward walking into and leaving dances. Parents pick up their kids, and lots of the popular kids pile up in vans. Most of the blonde and skinny girls look the same. I want my dad to pick me up. I miss his big, buff brown arms, the cool jazz he always has playing in his car.

At the end of the dance, Rachel Goldstein picked me up, her dumb folk music blaring from the dusty Volvo. I'm saying Rachel Goldstein instead of Mom because lately she is more like a cartoon character than a mother.

All of the dance nausea came back. I got into the car and she immediately started asking me questions about the dance. "Why aren't you with Abby? Did you dance, Franny? Blah, blah, blah!"

Her questions, the strobe light, the loud music, the cheap cologne I smelled all afternoon—it all caught up to me. I told my well-meaning but annoying mother that I was tired from dancing and needed to rest in bed. I ran into the bathroom like a maniac as soon as we pulled into the driveway. I pulled back my hair with a scrunchie, thinking I was going to throw up.

I was sure something would come out, but it didn't. I just spit a few times, watching my drool circle around the clean toilet bowl. I put on my music from my phone and jumped into bed. I pretended I was asleep when my mom walked in. Happy dumb Valentine's Day.

Twenty-Six

I DIDN'T MENTION THE OUTCOME OF the dog story yet because it's a very long story without a good ending. Bottom line—the Ziffs really didn't want Selma. There was finally a mediocre ending, but I got grounded for lying, and what made me feel the worst was telling the Ziffs untrue things. My mom explained the situation to my dad before I had the opportunity to. I overheard her telling my dad.

"Frances is pushing things too far. She lied about a dog in order to impress the librarian."

My mom must have also said something to Joanie in either an email or a phone call, because last week when I had an appointment, Joanie looked at me funny and said, "So, Frances, how was *your* week?" in a very knowing way. I could tell she wanted me to talk about it, mostly because of my being psychic, and also because my mother wants to control me and would probably handpick the topics I talk to Joanie about if she could. I'm actually certain that Joanie knew what transpired; she just wanted to hear it from me. If I'm the patient, shouldn't I pick the items we discuss, you know, like on a menu? I told her what happened, but just a short version of it. She asked me why I thought I wanted to push a dog on someone. I told her I didn't know, but that this librarian was my favorite person at my new school. "Would you feel okay if Mr. Ziff gave you a red sweater because he liked the color red?" she asked me, in like the sweetest voice ever. I told her I might feel weird, but I'd probably appreciate it. I'm pretty sure I later added that my friends and family might think it was strange, unless it was my birthday or something.

I told her, "I like how we discuss books and big words and stuff. He feels like family to me."

She smiled and leaned closer to me. "You see, you guys are good, you don't have to do extra. You have a good friendship."

I think I understood what she meant. We talked about losing animals; I hadn't talked about Stella in a long time. Joanie lost her dog named Cody. That still breaks her heart, even though she has another dog now. She showed me a picture of Cody in a silver frame. He was a medium-size yellow lab. I wonder if she talks about him to other patients, or just me. I like being in her office, walking straight to the humming sound of her aquarium at the start of each session.

Above the aquarium is a framed picture of her ex-husband, who incidentally is also black like me. He's really nice-looking for an older man, and Joanie says he comes from a family of eleven kids. She told me he's also part Jewish, just like me. So far, I like everything about Joanie. When she laughs, she throws her head back. I always look forward to our appointments because she listens to me, and also for the hot water dispenser I use to make tea in the waiting room. Joanie lets me have decaf tea with sweet vanilla cream in it. I like to hold a hot paper cup in my hands as we talk about stuff.

I don't know why, but I often find myself staring at this picture of her ex-husband. She told me a few sessions ago that James is her ex-husband but is still her very good friend. When I ask questions about him, she smiles and says that she isn't here to talk about her journey; she's here to support me with mine. The picture of James reminds me of my dad. Not because they are both black, but because they have similar jawlines and smiles. After I asked her a bunch of questions, adding an exaggeration that he looks really familiar, she told me that he's a gifted and well-known drummer named James Levi. He's played drums professionally all over the world. I'm very curious about him and can't help but want to know more about Joanie's personal life. I tell Joanie almost everything; shouldn't I know more things about her? She said my sessions are private unless I talk about hurting myself, others, illegal drugs, or drug-related activities.

I ended up bringing Selma to one of our sessions. I really like her and wish she could stay with our family, but I'm in enough trouble. I tell myself, You got her out of the SPCA, a great deed. The right person will take her, I just have to pray and not stress out. My mom gave me one week to find Selma a home, and I still can't see my friends or watch TV. During last week's ASB meeting, the vice principal told me to check in with the assisted living place a few miles away called Paradise Villa. He told me that they might like a dog like Selma. She is the sweetest animal I ever met and is more of a lap dog than anything. She never has accidents and rarely barks. I told my mom about the place, and surprisingly, someone she knows from the Parent's Center has a parent living there. So, the ending was not what I had as a plan, but now sweet Selma has a home and has the love of about twenty seniors with health and memory problems. She naps in the office and sometimes in residents' rooms, and goes home with the manager, Ana, who ended up adopting her.

I spent a lot of time processing this dog story with Joanie. She kind of makes me break things down when we talk about my intentions and my actions. Very often she says, "What does it look like to have a good day at school, Frances?" We continue to talk about Mom, Dad, Ingrid,

Frank, school, cliques, middle school drama, kind of everything. She asked me about boys, and I answered by telling her, "I want to wait until I'm older, but I want to date somebody mature who reads a lot."

Joanie agreed and said that some boys my age might seem very good-looking, but they're too young to make good decisions, and studies show they're impulsive.

"You're a heart person," she added. We agreed that middle school is a good time to have friends of all genders and to participate in fun activities in groups, staying open to new friendships and away from dating pressure.

She offered to invite my mom or brother to our sessions, but I told her I like private sessions. She said, "You're fine just the way you are, Frances. Can you repeat it back to me?"

I said, "I'm fine just the way I am."

In a loud voice and without blinking, Joanie said, "Do you like me, Frances?" I was kind of surprised by her question.

"Well, yes, you understand me," I answered quickly.

She started to laugh, and she raised her fist. "Well don't ya go out and surprise me with a dog, cuz the answer is *no*!" We both laughed. When I'm with Joanie, the clock is like a cartoon clock, nothing is real, time just runs wild.

One thing I'm really excited about is that in April I get to be in a Monday after-school program called the Word Lab. How cool that I get to be with seventh- and eighth-grade students and writing volunteers through the Young

Writers Program for ten weeks at the MAH, our downtown museum near Trader Joe's. We'll publish a real book that gets printed in July. The book will contain finished stories and poems from three sessions of students that attend our school. I get to keep one free copy, and Bookshop Santa Cruz, my favorite bookstore, will sell it! That teacher I mentioned, Wendy Thompson, encouraged me to get my paperwork signed and carpool information filled out so that I can for sure start in April. The genre is the permission to write anything we want, up to 750 words! I'm so stoked. Abby and Kylie are going also, as long as volleyball practice doesn't get in the way.

I'm not ashamed or proud, but I've now spent some time in the principal and vice principal's offices, once in February and once in March. I'll name my offenses "The Substitute Mishap" and "The Deviated Septum." Oy Vey.

So, in chronological order, we had a sub (or guest teacher as they're called in California) named Ms. Longsine in Core. She had a big rooster neck and funny, bleached gray/blonde hair. She wore a lot of blue eye shadow and had these greenish, lizard-like eyes. She had trouble unlocking the door when the first bell rang. She was carrying a cup of coffee, a long-strapped purse, and a tote bag, all which were systematically getting caught on the key chain holding her classroom key. She kept on dropping everything while unlocking the door. I offered to help her, which was a good thing because she really needed it. She spilled coffee on the roll sheet she was reading our names from, but either didn't notice or didn't care. I helped her pronounce the names correctly, which she really seemed to appreciate. Everyone was talking over her while she read the agenda. I heard her say, "Come on, guys. I was hoping to leave your teacher with a good report," a few times, but it was drowned out by our rowdy class. This always happens when we have guest teachers. I had never seen this sub before, and I had the feeling she was new.

The phone in the classroom was ringing, but the noise was so loud that I didn't think she heard it. I keep a whistle in my backpack, so to do her a favor and get everyone's attention I decided to blow it. Well, not to be too funny, but I guess I *blew it* just as everyone froze, and this one girl named Jasmine screamed at the top of her lungs and fell off her chair. The whole class started to laugh. Since arriving on campus, I don't think I ever got so many laughs and high-fives, so I have to admit it felt pretty epic. Screams and laughter did not please Ms. Longsine, to say the least. I tried to explain to the principal that I was only trying to help. I was told, "Frances, you made a poor choice. You took it too far."

I served two lunch detentions. I blew a whistle to help get my class to listen to the teacher, and this was my thanks?

Fast-forward to March 16. A regular day on the middle school campus. Another substitute, this time, a math class.

She was tall, very pale, maybe mid-forties; Donna Konnelly was her name. I've definitely seen her on campus and walking into the staffroom. I also helped her pronounce student names. She even said, "Thank you, Frances," when I corrected her on a few Hispanic surnames that I've memorized. She had a very unusual nose. One nostril appeared to be closed. It looked like a broken garage door. She had a very soft-spoken voice. A kid named Mario was making faces and pulling his nostrils out and laughing. I remembered drawing noses with my grandma a few summers back and vaguely recalling her say that noses were very difficult. She told me that even fine artists struggle with making noses, and they basically take a lot of practice.

I finished taking notes in math and grabbed one of the mini whiteboards that we use at our table groups. I began to draw noses. I wasn't drawing her nose; I was just drawing a nose at random. I was trying to recall how to start the nose sketch, and then after looking at this teacher, I remembered a term I once looked up. When one nostril protrudes more than the other, it's called a "deviated septum." Out of sheer boredom, I tried to remember how to spell it correctly. So I drew a nose and wrote *Deviated Septum* in my very best writing. The next thing I knew, this teacher gave me a referral and told me, "Making fun of people needs to be stopped before high school or you'll make enemies." She then added in a rather sad voice with a long sigh, "You started out so helpful to me;

what a shame." When she told me this, all I could do was focus on her nose, and I realized that she must have had at least one medical procedure to fix it, which actually fascinated me. I was looking for a scar but didn't see one. It was weird, but I just couldn't stop looking at her different nostrils.

I was sent to the vice principal's office, and the following was my apology letter I was asked to write.

Dear Mrs. Konnelly,

I apologize for drawing pictures that offended you. Nobody deserves to be made fun of, but I actually was not making fun of you. I am very sorry if you did not feel respected. I do respect you, and I am writing to you today to tell you how sorry I am. While I think that this is a misunderstanding, I think you are a terrific substitute teacher, and I hope to have you in another class soon.
With hope that you will forgive me,
Your friend,

Frances Green

The school counselor called my mom because this was my third referral. I'm grounded because my mom thinks I'm "going too far" to get laughs and shock value. She doesn't understand that I felt sorry for the guest teacher because she had no classroom control, like zero. My mom added, "You'll lose more privileges like your phone if you disrespect anyone again, got it, young lady?"

I told her that my plan was to do something good for my school, you know, to show who I really am. I forgot to mention that ASB made $260 profit from the Valentine's dance last month. I'm proud to say this! March still seems, however, to be the month that Frances either gets framed or gets into trouble just because she thinks outside of the boxes. I promise when I'm a parent I will not ground my kids; I'll simply listen to them.

My mother started Facebook around the start of the new year. She's managed to stay in touch with old friends from Boulder, her cousins in Brooklyn, etc.

Well, about a week ago, I couldn't help but notice that she only had about twelve friends. Of course she left her Facebook account open, so of course I was tempted. Do I think it was a big deal? Heck no. Does she? Oh yeah! All I did was send a friend request to Ingrid. Ingrid, who's very social, of course accepted, and what I didn't know and I know now is that you get a phone alert from Facebook when you become friends with a new person. This fell on the heels of my mother finding out that Abby and I cut our afternoon class, and of course my three referrals. I explained that my grades are good and that she should be proud that I've made friends, but the leash around my neck is getting shorter and shorter. She showed me the phone alert about Ingrid, and because it caught me off guard I started to sniffle and put my hands over my eyes, and in a very dramatic voice I said, "Mom, you never had a mother and a stepmother. I was just trying to bring the family together…"

She answered a pretty good line. "If I want to be friends with Ingrid, let me initiate. You *have no* right to invade my privacy and pretend to be me."

I really had no comebacks to this one. I told her she could unfriend her, and then she got all psycho again, so we both decided to let it be. When I told my dad, he thought it was kind of cute. Anyway, I cleaned out my mom's car, folded Frank's clothes, and continue to vehemently apologize. I'm grounded for two days, and as soon as I come home from school I have to put my phone in a basket next to the door and can only use it at school for emergencies.

The afternoon I cut class, Abby and I jogged to West Cliff and went people watching. I showed my mom my sketches and descriptions of people I saw on our little field trip—but I soon found out it wasn't going to get me out of the doghouse.

Other than getting in trouble for meddling and being the true artist I was born to be by doing creative things, my life is still going fairly well in Santa Cruz. I'm still swimming and practicing piano, getting money for organizing and doing childcare. I spend time alone after dinner, usually. I'm still having trouble sleeping. Joanie asks me why, but I don't really know. I think I came out of the womb with insomnia. I just wonder about things, and before I know it another hour or so have passed. I was sneaking on my phone at night, but now my mom takes it and charges it in her room. I wrote this the other night:

INSOMNIA

Wednesday's moon
3 am
My old friend insomnia is sleeping over again
You don't bring me distress, you don't bring me delight
You are a bark without a bite
I roll over, offering you a fight
You are an awfully long P.S.
So I think of butter and bread
and everything nobody said
You are pink and green and blue and red
When I am tired, I am yawning
And baby salmon are spawning
And a new day is dawning
I am black from Boulder
And white from California
A swimmer and an organizer
A psychic candle hoping her dad can see her flame from across the mountain ranges that separate them

I'm so psyched! I started the Word Lab and I'm working on short memoir writing and poetry. My WPA (writing project assistant) is named David, and he's a retired psychology professor from UCSC. He likes my writing and is really smart and kind. I like that there are other people in our class I didn't know before, like an eighth grader named Azula, who reads as much as I do, and two other eighth-grade students named J.T. and Skylar. They read aloud a great narrative on non-binary people and asked the afternoon Word Lab session students and writing assistants to please start using *they* instead of automatically assuming *he* or *she*.

Sometimes Wendy drives a few of us, and sometimes other parents do. I haven't decided on what I want to write about for the published piece, but it's so inspiring to be around other writers. Last week we watched a video that Kurt Vonnegut made about the shape of stories. I really needed something to look forward to after school on Mondays. I love writing in the art chamber of the museum, and sometimes David lets our group of five sit on the stairs of the museum to do our freewrites. The museum is closed to the public on Mondays, so it's like being in a special club. Often I can't sleep because poetry wakes me up.

Twenty-Seven

I WENT TO THE DOCTOR LAST WEEK to update my papers for sports and got measured. I am five-foot-nine. I don't remember exactly what I weigh, but somewhere around 165 pounds. I don't like when girls my age trip about how much they weigh. I eat all of the time, whatever I want, and I just exercise. I think people who are too skinny don't look good. They also don't look healthy. My grandma says the trick is just to feel good in your skin. I do. Abby is short and says she wishes she could be tall like me. I just wish my braces would come off. I have a big gap between my two front teeth, and my bottom teeth are pretty jacked up, but my new orthodontist said by next Christmas they should be off. Her name is Dr. Ariana, and she is really sweet and pretty. Her dad is another dentist in the office, and her mom works at the front desk. I think that's pretty cool. She is a dentist and orthodontist. I wish I could invent something huge like completely invisible braces that don't hurt in my lifetime.

I turned a dozen years on the seventeenth of April. My birthday was on a Thursday. I ate a tuna sandwich and played chess during lunch at game club in the library. We ran out of time, but I had this boy named Ramon's queen, and I was in the lead. Abby and I rode bikes to my house after school. It felt liberating not to be grounded anymore. My grandma made a cake for me, and I snuck Abby into the gym so we could swim. About 5:00 p.m. we changed clothes and got ready for my birthday sushi dinner at a place called Akira's. My mom left me a text that she had to lead a family group and would meet us at the restaurant at 6:30. My grandma took me, Abby, Frank, and one of my eighth-grade friends named Hector. He lives by the grocery store near the school, so we picked him up on the way.

We sat down at the table, and because the crew at Akira knows Frank they gave him a free soda and let him sit at the bar so he could watch the sushi rolls being made.

We were just ordering the edamame and shrimp appetizers when suddenly somebody put their hands over my eyes from behind me. Everything became still and quiet. I'll never forget this feeling as long as I live. I heard Abby and maybe another voice saying, "Shhh!" as I just felt this warmth on my eyes. I squinted and could tell that the hand had a ring and a watch on it, and it was a brown hand. The smell was a familiar musk cologne scent. I knew that smell. I knocked over my water, spun around and yelled, “Dad!” I was shaking and kept on saying, "OH MY GOD!”

I thought I was going to hyperventilate!

My mom smiled and my grandma had tears in her eyes. My dad was laughing a lot, and then Frank came over to our table. My dad told him to give me a hug, and he sort of touched my back and said, “Happy birthday, Frances,” in the same tone he always uses. It was the best surprise ever having my dad show up!

We took a lot of pictures and pigged out on shrimp tempura and sushi. After that we had some mocha ice cream on top of my grandma’s killer vanilla cake. The wait staff sang “Happy Birthday,” and Abby and Hector seemed to be bonding with my dad. My dad told me later that night that he was asked to speak at San Jose State University and wanted to surprise me by showing up on my birthday. He was staying at the Hotel Equinox and would fly home on Sunday. He rented a car, but my mom picked him up at the hotel so I wouldn’t see him. I’m one lucky girl. Life sure got better!

I talked my parents into taking Friday off, with the caveat of course, as long as I do my homework over the weekend. We all piled in my mom’s car at the end of the night as my parents were taking turns telling stories about me when I was a kid. It was cool seeing them get along so well.

The next day I went to my dad's lecture. It was very long, but also kind of interesting. It was a PowerPoint lecture and then a Q&A (question and answer) about inclusion in special education. I think I want to start a blog about being a sister to someone who has autism.

People have always asked me about it, so I figure I'll just tell the truth. For one thing, I don't like when people stare at my brother. That's the first thing to mention. Just don't stare at people who are different; it's simply not cool. Another thing is, I just want to know about Frank's personal feelings. He doesn't talk about them; at least I never heard him. I overheard him telling Mitchell that Rosie, from his work, is "gorgeous", but when I asked him about her, he said, "I don't know." He spends time with Mitchell and a few others, but I don't think they talk about feelings and stuff like I do with Abby, but who knows? I'm not around him 24/7. I respect my brother, and he respects me. He does say, "Frances, you are always writing." I think writing is really good for most people, but Frank does *not* like to write; he never has. Dad says he'll probably take coding classes either in high school, college, or trade school.

I like to write because I can say whatever I want and get my feelings out. The good ones, the bad ones, the ugly ones. People will judge you, but paper and blank screens on computers won't. I can't understand why Frank and others don't like to write. It seems the kids who are really good at math don't really like to write, and kids like me who love to write find math hard or not very interesting. I don't mind the idea of math, especially because it's so concentrated and organized. There is a "however," however. I don't like that there is only one answer. Mr. Ziff helps me with math, but honestly I forget what he tells me and what my math teachers tell me from day to day. I learned my times tables really fast, but I think that's because I'm wired to be organized and I enjoy patterns. Word problems piss me off, if you really want to know. I get them wrong on tests, but not because I don't understand them. They ask you questions in a backward way. The way teachers say them, it's like a flytrap. They want you to get caught. They want you to guess the wrong answer.

Joanie asked me if I get less attention because Frank is a special-needs kid. She asked me a few times. Once I pretended I didn't really hear her because I felt kind of nervous or something. Sometimes I don't think or realize I'm nervous, but my palms sweat and my heart starts beating really fast. When I play basketball, like I often do, I *know* my heart will go fast and so I expect it to. But to the contrary, sometimes when Joanie asks me things or my Core teacher pulls my name out of the bundle of equity sticks to answer a question, I get kind of stressed or nervous. My answer to Joanie's question about getting less attention than Frank is actually a yes, but it depends on if we are talking about my mom or dad. My mom gives me plenty of attention—maybe too much. She doesn't really know how to talk to Frank. I have heard her say that when she drinks wine with her therapist friends. She takes everything personally, so probably she thinks she isn't doing things right. As far as my dad goes, I guess he gives me less attention. I wouldn't want him to know this, but it's true. I obviously read a lot, and I remember once trying to read his thesis on autism. I understood some of it, but not all. There was research done about people with autism having different brains than neurologically typical people. I worry that my brain is boring to him. Deep down, he couldn't help but love Frank more than me. Isn't it weird that both my old therapist Michelle from Boulder *and* Joanie asked me the exact same question? Maybe they went to the same college for therapists!

I don't really fight with Frank directly, at least not in the sense that people talk about with sibling rivalry, but Frank is the topic of most of our family drama. My parents used to fight about Frank all the time. I pretended to be asleep in the car a few times. My mom wanted him to follow the rules more and would get really emotional at his special education meetings. My dad, on the other hand, always wanted the teachers and aides to let him be free and do what comes naturally. My brother is awesome; I just don't really know him. I know Abby really well because we talk about everything. I used to talk with my friend Billy in the same best-friend way. Maybe I just need to like Frank exactly how he is. On a Saturday afternoon a couple of weeks back when my dad was here, the three of us walked on West Cliff. West Cliff is one of my favorite places to walk in Santa Cruz, and my dad kept on hearing about it so he said, "Take your old man to your happy place, Franny!"

We parked by Natural Bridges Beach and ate bean and cheese burritos on the large rocks. Frank had a pair of binoculars and was looking for whales. This pretty lady in tight yellow shorts was jogging in front of us, and I just knew my dad would notice her. I thought about what my grandma said, that "Kevin always had a wandering eye." It's kind of a funny expression, like someone has a loose or detached eyeball. Anyway, my dad was looking straight at this jogger. It was kind of random, but my dad asked me in a whisper, "Does Frank have a girlfriend?"

I told him, "No, not that I know of. Why don't you ask him yourself, Dad?"

Frank was scrunching up his face, holding the binoculars really close. His tongue was kind of hanging out of his mouth like a thirsty lizard. "Hey, Frankie, do you have a girlfriend?" he asked in a playful tone. Then he added, "Your family here wants to know."

No answer. This is very typical. It takes him a few times to actually answer questions. The same question was asked, no response. Frank gets deep into whatever he's doing. Finally, I told my dad to bring it up to him when we're driving back in the car. He hasn't been around Frank for some time. Maybe he forgot that if things don't work with Frank, you should just try it later.

He gave me a funny look. "Once again, you're right, kiddo. Why would he want to talk to me when he's looking for whales?"

I feel impatient sometimes. I know when my dad visits we'll mostly have a good time. I'm writing this chapter a few weeks after he left. It takes me a while to want to write, even though in my mind I have a lot to say. I overheard my mom telling Grandma Harriet that I'm very moody. She even used the word *snotty*. I hate that word. I'm not a booger on a napkin that people blow their nose into. I just feel impatient because I know I'll be in a bad mood when my dad leaves again. Why do dads leave? Why do moms leave? Nobody should be forced to stay married. I just wish people got along better or were forced to take a test before they got married. Divorce is necessary, I suppose, but it just makes me feel irritable.

I don't necessarily want my parents to get back together, or for Gary or Ingrid to go away, but the whole thing just annoys me. I tried to explain it to Joanie one day in therapy, but I just felt like looking at the fish in her aquarium and didn't want to answer a million bazillion questions about anger or sadness as it relates to divorce. I'm not sad! I'm not angry! I'm impatient and I don't know why.

As the weather gets colder and I get more used to California, I start to miss Boulder more and more. Mostly I daydream about my dad and the parks I played in near the Pearl Street Mall. My mom says I'm acting sarcastic and seem depressed. My grades are pretty good so far, but I feel like a robot sometimes. I'm doing what I am supposed to do, but I don't feel motivated or sparked other than in my writing group every Monday. My face in the mirror often looks bored.

Twenty-Eight

A MONTH OR SO AFTER MY DAD flew back to Boulder, I was going through my mom's Volvo at the gas station near my house. I was annoyed by the empty water bottles, sticky notes with scribbles on them, and sandy leashes on the floor of the front seat. Okay, I may have also been kind of snooping. Shh! My absentminded mother was picking at her nails while fishing through her purse for a credit card to use for getting gas. After she found it and started pumping gas, I was doing what I usually do at the gas station, wiping the windows with the squeegee and recycling water bottles. My mother is so dang messy.

The song "Free Bird" was playing at the gas station, and I thought about the last time I heard it. I was at my dad's apartment after he moved out, and we were playing chess. Anyway, I started missing him. I watched my mom fumble to put the gas handle back on its stand. I watched her clumsy body carefully and completely, the way a student would study or memorize a math problem. My mom isn't steady on her feet. My dad is smooth. He is like a dancer, and she is like somebody after they have surgery on their butt. He holds his head high, and she looks at things as if she is constantly puzzled, like people are machines and she can't understand their function. This is my own interpretation, but I don't know how they ever met in the middle and got married and had sex and two children named Frank and Frances. Can you tell I'm in kind of a bad or irritable mood?

So after we got gas, we were on our way to the store to get some tortillas and cheese for dinner. I was thinking about what I wanted for dessert and at the same time thinking about the science words I was studying for an upcoming test. My mom was picking at her chin, and this time I couldn't help but blurt out, "You're picking at your skin. Why don't you look in the mirror and see that you're making marks on yourself?"

She started to adjust the mirror, leaning close to the windshield. Suddenly, CRASH! I got slammed forward and heard brakes being slammed and then terrible honking. My mom had rear-ended the car in front of us. It happened in the blink of an eye, just like how people explain it. The noise was horrible. Horrible and haunting. The airbag was deployed, and a few things fell forward from the backseat. We were both okay, but my neck hurt and I felt dizzy. Cars were going around us, staring.

The driver of the white Honda that my uncoordinated mother hit was a young college girl with a pierced lip. She had a ton of books in her front seat and had really pretty blue eyes and wore a beanie. She kind of had a lisp and kept saying, "Whoa, this never happened before. I'm from Chicago."

Her car seemed to have damage to the bumper and trunk area. A nice police officer with crooked bottom teeth and an expensive-looking gold watch took the report. He asked me, "Are you okay?"

I answered that I was. I just wanted to go home and jump under the covers. I was embarrassed and pissed off at my mom. Why didn't I just stay home? Why does she have to be so lame?

The police officer, named Officer Adams, asked my mom if she was texting. "She doesn't even answer the phone if she's in the car," I responded. I didn't want my mom to get into trouble. He said to me, "She can answer my question without help, thank you," and began writing things on a pad of paper. She was shaking like a nervous wreck. Her hands were trembling so badly that I had to find her auto insurance card in that pouch thingy in her glove box. There was a big crack in the windshield, but it didn't shatter. We were just down the street from the gas station. I had to walk away from the scene of the crime because I knew I'd say something mean to my mom, and Joanie once said to count to ten or take a quick walk to calm down. My mother is a terrible driver and now everyone will know this.

I tied my shoe and sat down on a curb. I started crying. A lady carrying a laundry basket said, "Are you okay?"

I said, "Yeah, I'm okay. Thanks." I didn't want to talk to anybody. I thought about all of the times I noticed my mom picking at her face or her nails, and that maybe it was foreshadowed, like in books and movies. Perhaps I knew somehow that something bad would happen. Why can't she just get gas like a normal mom? Why did this crappy thing have to happen? Where's my dad when I need him? I decided to walk back to the car. The officer was still there talking to my mom and this lady from Chicago. They were all nodding their heads like it was a game show. My neck was hurting and I didn't want to even look at my mom. We never went to the store to get food for dinner.

My grandma said we could borrow her car for a week or so while it was in the shop, and Gary brought Chinese food over. I went to my grandma's and she rubbed my feet as we watched *The Voice*.

Whenever I think of April, I'll try to superimpose my happy birthday memories of my dad surprising me, but I'm afraid I'll always be forced to recall this traumatic fender bender. It just bums me out.

Twenty-Nine

AS IT TURNS OUT, FRANK DOES have a girlfriend, and her name is Rosie. She's a cashier at Best Buy. The only thing is, she doesn't know that she's Frank's girlfriend. We're talking first crush. He told us that she has pretty red lipstick and she speaks both Spanish and English. They ride the bus together from Harbor High. "She is nice and smacks her gum. She wears big hoop earrings, and also a silver cross necklace." This is how Frank describes her, very factual.

School is going so-so. Basketball is over now, so I'm not rushing around so much. I finished writing poetry for the Young Writers Program in the Word Lab, and the book will be published in July. David, my writing tutor, invited me and my mom to the temple he and his wife attend. She used to be a teacher at my school. I liked the music at Rock

Shabbat and hope to go back. Abby continues to be a good friend, but again, I don't like the friends she likes. We took my dogs on a walk yesterday. We were walking behind my school near the garden area when I noticed a man with a gray hoodie standing near the fence. I told Abby he looked like he was up to no good. He was holding something, but I couldn't tell what it was. I turned around, and the man seemed to be gone. There was a soccer game going on, and a bunch of people were watching. I noticed this same man standing near some bushes, apparently texting or doing something with his phone. He looked in our direction, possibly—

Abby said, "God Frances, that guy can tell you're watching him. Why are you staring?"

Abby and I didn't really get into a fight, but she told me that it bugs her when I stare people down. I tried to explain that I get feelings about people and that I'm usually right. She told me that I've been acting different, and so I told her the same thing. I caught myself sighing. I had biked to her house the day after the car crash and told her the ordeal. I said, "Can you believe my mom is this stupid? She rear-ended someone in broad daylight because she was looking in the mirror and not paying attention."

Abby was spreading peanut butter on pieces of celery, and in a really bored voice she responded with something like, "Well, at least nobody got hurt. She probably feels bad. Just let it go, Frances, it's really not a big deal. I'm sure your mom's insurance will pay for the other car." And that was that. She really didn't seem to care that I was in the car and how embarrassing it was. I sent her a text later that night about feeling traumatized by the car crash, and she never responded. I guess it's something I save for Joanie. If this happened to Abby, I mean, if she got into a car accident, I'd be making her dinner and sending her flowers.

I was thinking about this when Abby told me I was acting different. Really?

Abby and I didn't talk for a few minutes. We turned around at the corner of Poplar Street, the same street my school is on. I looked for the man again, but he wasn't around. I knew that I'd seen him before. He is medium height and really skinny. He wears these big high-top Converse tennis shoes and doesn't tie his shoelaces. He doesn't have good posture; his shoulders are kind of rounded, and he has a funny-shaped nose. I was getting this bad feeling about him, but at the same time trying to think of something clever to say to Abby in order to make things better. She was texting somebody and then abruptly said, "I'm going to get picked up soon by my dad."

"Are you mad at me?" I asked as we put the dogs' leashes away and walked inside my house.

"No," she said. "I just don't like when you stare at people. It's creepy."

I reminded her that I was a writer, that I notice crap that

others don't. She said, "Whatever," under her breath. Abby says that word when things bother her. I don't like the word *whatever*. I eavesdrop on my mom's phone calls with clients and have learned the expression, "passive-aggressive." To me, *whatever* is passive-aggressive because it's like someone shrugging their shoulders, but you can tell they're mad and not saying why.

I sat on my bed and started to read *Of Mice and Men*. Sometimes I feel like I'm wasting my big words on people who have never heard them. In chapter four, I found the word *contemptuously*, which triggered my imagination for the rest of the afternoon. Words mean so much to me. Mr. Ziff told me I should be in the spelling bee, and he gives me attention because I know how to use big words correctly. He's my favorite person at school to talk to. I think it's so cool that he sometimes rides his bike to school.

Anyway, back to Abby. Her dad came and got her about ten minutes later. Her parents are also divorced. Her mom is a lot friendlier than he is. He hardly looks at me and always tells Abby to hurry up. Abby and I were both looking at our phones, not really talking when she left.

I read a few more chapters, hoping to visit Salinas soon—it's close to Santa Cruz—because I want to see where Steinbeck lived. Later on I listened to some music. I like Adele. I turned it up pretty loud and started to look back again on the writing I started when I first left Boulder. It seems like I don't write much when things are good. I think when people's lives are good they're bumbling about like fancy people at rich dinner parties. They're not melancholy and thinking about everything, dissecting every cell and emotion. It feels more honest to write when things are making you sad or upset.

Anyway, I spent a full hour or so going through my leather-bound journal as well as the chapters on my laptop. Feelings are like cars at the carwash, one after another. After a while, every single car and every single customer looks and acts the same. Every customer wants a good-looking clean car. Feelings are really the same thing. Everyone works hard to get good feelings. Once I actually get into the groove of writing, it feels freeing, just like swimming, but it's not easy to start writing. I procrastinate my writing even though it's my most favorite thing to do in the whole world. I may have mentioned this, but I have one bad habit. I have bushy eyebrows. I tried to use a tweezer to pluck some hairs, but I made it uneven, which bugged me even more. When I was packing for the big move to California, I sat up on the counter and tried to shape my eyebrows with my mom's razor. It looked 65 percent good, and 35 percent ridiculous. My bad habit is touching my eyebrows. I find myself compulsively pushing them up and down and sideways. If I feel a stub of hair growing back it drives me crazy, and I have to pluck it out. If I really had to give a number of how often I tweeze or look at my eyebrows in the mirror, it's about four or thirty-five times a day.

Sometimes watching Netflix or reading a good book seems a whole lot better than writing in my journal or on my laptop, but there's a saying with writing I heard somewhere. The deeper you go, the freer you'll feel.

Thirty

I DON'T KNOW WHY, BUT I KEEP reliving the horrible sound and memory of my mother hitting the car. It's almost like I can't get it out of my head. My mom shouldn't have been picking, and I should've kept my mouth shut, but it started with her bad habit, and honestly she should've just been driving, just that one thing. The idea of driving makes me feel anxiety, but I like the idea of freedom that driving must entail.

Lately I feel nervous, like my adrenaline is pumping extra fast. I feel lonesome for something, but I don't know exactly what it is. I miss Boulder, mostly my dad and Billy. I called Billy, but he didn't answer the phone. My mom and my grandma knocked on my door and asked me if I wanted to make a cake with them. I didn't. I just felt like being alone on this windy Saturday. Last weekend was super fun. I spent the night at The Tannery with Abby, and we're finally getting along better. We biked to the Pacific Garden Mall, which is downtown. It is also where Joanie's office is. We locked up our bikes near Starbucks and bought two hot chocolates with extra whipped cream. We planted ourselves on a white metal bench and began the game we invented a few weeks ago called "PW and W." That stands for Pick Who and Where. We take turns picking out random people, and the other person has to find a name for the person, as well as at least one thing about them, like what they do for a living and where they're going.

I picked a random walker who was about twenty years old. He was walking fast while he held a Jamba Juice cup and looked at his cell phone. Abby said, "His name is Willy and he's taking a coding class at the community college called Cabrillo. He is meeting his cousin for lunch to help her understand her new iPhone."

Abby and I always laugh a lot when we play this game. I like making up things about people more than anything. We saw a lot of goth-looking people with dyed black hair and really skinny jeans that hung down low. I don't really go for this look, but the style is interesting. Abby and I both agreed that these are rich kids from the Midwest who are rebelling from their families. They are here in California, hitchhiking around to follow heavy metal band concerts.

Abby and I played this game for a few hours and then

got a slice of pizza and iced tea with extra sugar. I wondered what Abby would say about me if I was walking down the street. When I asked Abby, she looked up at the sky for a minute and replied, "I don't know, Frances. For sure, I would think you were fifteen or sixteen and your name would be more ethnic, like Kiandra or Iesha."

I thought that was very cool. "Where would I be going?" I really wanted to know.

"You'd be going to a natural food store like New Leaf, and you'd buy an avocado and coconut incense. After that, you'd go to the shoe store to buy black high-top tennis shoes."

Abby sometimes calls me "Avocado Chick" because she says I'm obsessed with avocadoes. I take them to school and eat them at home a lot. I put them on bagels, chips, and sandwiches I take to school.

Of course, Abby asked me the same question. That's my Abby; it's fair game. She'd have to know what I'd say about her.

I answered, "Your name is Anastasia, and you're walking to Bookshop Santa Cruz to buy an art book and a sketching pad. You're so boy crazy, though, that you end up walking into a tree because you're staring at some guy!"

At that, Abby proceeded to give me a karate chop on my back. I returned her violent act by twisting her arms until she screamed. Some people walking by started staring at us, which of course got us into a fit of laughing hysterics. We took a couple of selfies after we caught our breath again, and then arm in arm we walked to Marini's candy store to buy sour gummies.

On Sunday I filled out my reading log, played chess on the computer, took a nap, and then decided to clean my phone screen and case. When I looked at my phone, I saw that Billy called me back. I texted him, and we made a plan to talk after he ate dinner. We talked for forty-two minutes. We had the most intense talk *ever*! I told you that Billy tells me things he doesn't share with others. As Billy spilled his guts out to me, I took fast notes, mostly abbreviating words. I didn't want to forget anything. I talk about him in therapy with Joanie, and it was important that I relate this conversation to her as accurately as humanly possible.

Billy first apologized to me. He said something like, "Fran, I'm sorry if I was distant. I know I wasn't much fun over Christmas. I had a big science fair my parents were on me about. So, I'm sorry."

I told him not to worry about anything. I remember an awkward standstill on the phone, because I suddenly sneezed, and it broke the silence. Billy said, "I have something to tell you." He brought up a teacher named Ed Schuler that all of the students love. He's partially blind and brings his German shepherd service dog named Garvey everywhere he goes. He did long-term subbing in my fourth-grade class when my teacher went on maternity leave, and Billy said he's taking over his English class for the semester for some reason. Anyway, Ed plays this game with students called "Two Truths and a Lie." Basically, you take turns being "it" and you say three things; two of them will be false, and one will be true. You keep a straight poker face as you say the three things about yourself, so as not to throw off your audience. It's super fun, Billy said.

"Okay, so we finished our English quiz early, and Mr. Schuler started the first round by going first. We were curious about his personal life, being blind and all. We found out he protested in Vietnam and lost part of his eyesight in an explosion. And then it was my turn."

The phone was quiet again. "Billy, you still there?" I asked.

He totally had me looped in. "Yeah," he said, and then very quietly, "it just feels awkward is all."

He took a deep breath.

"Okay, I said these three things, Franny. I once rode a camel, I think I'm gay, and my father is a pilot."

I felt goose bumps on my arm. I knew I'd get this answer right.

"You never rode a camel, right?"

I said it without hesitating.

"Bingo, sister," he said in a happy voice. He suddenly sounded strong and proud, his voice louder, deeper.

"Did you tell your parents?" I asked carefully.

"After we hang up, I'm going to talk to my mom. My dad's been working a lot. It'll be easier to talk with my mom first, I think," Billy said. It sounded like he was eating popcorn or chips or something.

"Are you nervous?" I asked him.

"No, not really. I talked to Ed after class for a few minutes. He said I showed courage for being in touch with who I am inside."

He asked me toward the end of the conversation if I always knew he was gay. He said I was one of his best friends. I said, "Same."

He seemed to be waiting on the other end for something more. "Well, you told me at Red Rocks that your aunt thought you might be gay, but I didn't think much about it."

"But—did you *think* I was gay?" He pronounced *think* in a bold tone.

"Okay, then yes," I said. I had the feeling he was looking for reassurance.

We talked about other random things, people in Boulder, etc., but I just kept wishing that he'd come for a visit. I missed him. I'd take him downtown and to the beach every chance we got.

I told Joanie about our phone call at my next session. She was glad I was there for him. Billy is my most mature friend, for sure. I remember when I first met Joanie I told her that I prefer adults to my peers. I remember the conversation.

"Do you think that's weird?" I asked. I was doodling on my sketchpad when I asked her.

She moved close to me, scooting her chair super close. "No," she responded. We had intense eye contact. Her eyes swallowed me, but I stared right back at her, as if there was going to be a prize I'd win if I didn't blink. She kind of has this yellow ring around her iris. Maybe it was the question itself, or maybe it was from staring at her for so long, but I teared up. She handed me a Kleenex, but I pushed it away. I kind of knew I was starting to cry, but I didn't want to and pretended it wasn't there.

"No," she repeated, not picking up the small blue box of Kleenex I had just knocked over.

"Well, most people think it's weird," I told her.

She got into my face and very gently told me, "I'll answer your questions honestly."

At the end of my session, she told me that she also preferred the company of older people when she was my age.

I asked her why it took so long to grow up. She gave me what seemed to be another honest answer. She threw her hands up in bewilderment.

I always thought that Billy and I would make the best college roommates. He makes me think about stuff and I'm really happy he came out to me.

Thirty-One

WELL, I'M ALMOST A SEVENTH GRADER. Mr. Arnold thanked me again for watching some little kids the other night while they held a meeting about the eighth-grade graduation dance. The more he compliments me, the more I want to help out my school. I was walking around campus at lunch with him, just talking about stuff. I feel like I can say anything to him and he won't judge me. He and his partner have one of their boys at our school, but I think he's in the dual immersion Spanish class, so I don't see him that much.

The sun was out and I was in a good mood. I mentioned to him that Billy was going to come out to his parents about being gay. He said the same thing that Ed did, about being brave and all. As we were chatting about TV shows, graduation practice, and just random stuff, some kid threw his apple in the quad, and so once again my good talks with teachers and principals got interrupted.

I could feel my mood shifting quickly. Why are so many lame middle school kids so freaking immature? I can't even think or write about how much it bugs me without my blood literally boiling inside my body. Don't these dummies know that they can swim or hit a punching bag or kick a soccer ball to get their energy out? I hate littering. The earth is so giving and generous and heartbreakingly beautiful. Throwing an apple when the trash can is right there, like five feet away. Really? Dammit, really? I was livid. I was so frustrated I could almost cry on demand, so I walked away. I told Mr. Arnold that I was meeting a friend and had to go.

I decided to go down the hallway to game club and took a deep breath. I went to the bathroom and saw some girl putting eyeliner on. When she walked away I quickly glanced in the mirror, making myself a forced cheesy smile. It wasn't a real smile, but it would have to suffice for now. I flung the library door open with all of my might. I had fourteen minutes to play chess. I asked a girl from El Salvador if she wanted to play. She had a book in her hand, but I could tell from her eyes that she wasn't really reading it.

She said, "Okay," in a teeny tiny soft voice, and we took the chess pieces out of the plastic bag together, and I set up the black pieces. She nodded at me to start. I moved my horse; it is always my first move, in case you're wondering. She was looking at my necklaces, I could tell. I wear two: the Star of David and a cross. I wear it with the assurance that people will wonder about me. Is Frances Jewish or Catholic or Christian?

I didn't know how much English she knew because she is in the Newcomer English Core class, but I said, "Me gusta Dios," which I think is "I like God."

She nodded her head and moved her third pawn on the right two spaces forward. She had little tiny teeth and her foot was shaking nervously. She wore a pink sweatshirt that had a Nike symbol and tight blue jeans and black tennis shoes. She made a few moves that threw me off a bit, and I have to admit that I was distracted by a cute boy playing chess at the table behind me and wasn't that focused on our game after a few minutes. I figured I had more experience than she did, so my guard was down. One of the math teachers who supervises the lunchtime game club made an announcement: of only a few minutes left before the end of lunch. The bell was going to ring, and nobody won, but we both took each other's queens.

I wanted to try to speak Spanish with her, but my braces hurt from being tightened the other day, and I like to be really quiet when I play chess. I try to hear my opponent thinking. I was thinking about that gypsy woman at the Renaissance festival telling me that I'm psychic. I try to guess where the next move will be whenever I play chess. Sometimes when I get really into playing, I pretend to leave my body. I think of myself as a very smart cell, or a bodiless spirit lurking about. As I waited for the girl to move, I started tapping my fingers on the table. I moved my index finger from side to side while squinting my eyes, which is a new habit I'm forming when I tune in.

I was recalling a dream that I had the night before. It was so freaking real. The more I moved my finger, the clearer my dream became. In my dream, with the same finger, I was flipping the garbage disposal switch off and on. I was running water in my dad's sink and noticed that Ingrid's head was stuck in the drain. I turned on the water with full force, and there she was, her wet hair spraying water everywhere. She was yelling, "Frances," really loudly, and I was drowning out her voice and face with the disposal. She would go away, and then somehow always reappear. I kept trying to recall more from the dream when suddenly the girl cleared her throat to get my attention.

"Your turn," she said with a strong Spanish accent. I could no longer focus on the game, and our time was up anyway. I shook hands with this girl, and we put the chess pieces back in the Ziploc bag. After lunch was over, I stayed in the library like I always do every fifth period. I noticed a handwritten xeroxed paper on Mr. Ziff's desk.

Chromebook # 24 Missing Since Spring Break.

Last Seen in the Innovation Center. REWARD!

I started tapping my fingers on the desk. I put back the books from the cart and checked some books out to people, but mostly I was getting psychic hits about this laptop. I continued tapping the table I was sitting at, stretching out my hands. My fingernails are painted a soft blue; I could almost get lost in their color, as if I'm in a misty forest. I twisted my three silver and turquoise rings so that the front of the rings were facing. I turned my neck until it popped and began staring at the clock. I stared so hard that the numbers no longer looked like numbers. My mind suddenly zeroed in on that day I took the picture of two guys trying to open a lock in the Innovation Center, and I couldn't help but start thinking about the man I saw recently with the hoodie and the unlaced high tops.

About three months had passed, but when I get a psychic hit, I pay attention. "Mr. Ziff, I think I know something about the Chromebook, you know, number twenty-four," I said a few minutes later as I was wiping down the computer monitors.

He kind of bit his lip and told me it was a shame, but added, "You never know; it might show up. Have you seen it, Frances?" He wiped a shiny red apple on his plaid shirt. I watched him take a big bite out of it, and with amazement I witnessed him chew and wipe his mouth at the same time. "Sorry I'm eating in front of you; I wish I had another one to offer you," he added.

I told him, "No, it's fine. I'm not hungry, but I think I saw a suspicious character hanging out by the Innovation Center not too long ago. I have his picture on my phone."

After I said that I explained in my proudest voice that I have a sixth sense and feel things strongly. I figured that it was meant to be, back in April, when my mom plowed into the car in front of her. It shook me up so that I could be more aware of my surroundings, and I was sure that I was watching the guy with the hoodie for a good reason. It was starting to add up. I added that I was usually right with my intuition. Mr. Ziff was chewing the hell out of this apple core by now and looked amused. "Go let Admin know then, Frances. I hope you can help relocate this. It's very expensive to replace our laptops."

I felt as though maybe this opportunity happened so that I could be the hero I always wanted to be.

Mr. Ziff will tell his friends outside of school that, using her special detective powers, his beloved fifth-period aide found the person who stole the laptop. I'll get out of math tests in order to teach people how to take pictures of suspects without them knowing, and if possible I'll give instructions to others on how to zoom in on and enhance psychic awareness. My mom and my grandma will take me out to buy new leggings and maybe a skateboard. I'll be on the news, and this creepy guy will return the computer and go to jail. My dad will be really proud and he might even teach me how to drive. These feelings were overpowering me. This was so exciting!

I asked permission from Mr. Ziff to get my phone out of my backpack, and I carefully scrolled through my last five months or so of pictures. It was a speedy blur of faces and images; every color and facial expression could be accounted for. I easily had 400 pictures to scroll through. I looked for the section of pictures that came after my five days in Boulder, which was in December. There were pictures of Chloe and my dad and Ingrid, Billy, our Benjamin ficus Hanukkah tree, Gary and my mom, Frank, Mitchell, and suddenly, there were the three pictures I was searching for.

I got really overjoyed to find the one I remembered taking. This picture brought back distant memories. It was Abby on a computer in the Innovation Center at school, smiling with Elijah the teacher standing next to her and showing her how to make shadows. The next was a framed picture of a bee that a student had made, and then, finally, the picture I needed—the picture of two men crouching down in the small room with the computer carts. I zoomed in on this picture, my heart pounding like rolling thunder. It was the guy with the shaved head that piqued my curiosity, actually hitting it out of the ballpark. I imagined this man to be the same dude I saw again with Abby that Saturday near school, the one who Abby had noticed I was staring at.

The picture I took of him was taken from too far away,

but it could easily have been the same person. Although this man was bent over, I imagined he was about five-ten. He had a neatly trimmed mustache and goatee in this picture. He was wearing a greenish jacket and jeans. The man I saw with Abby had a goatee for sure, but I wasn't certain about the mustache. It all seemed to make sense, the fact that I took a picture of this purely on instinct. The fact that I'm Mr. Ziff's aide, and it's my first year to prove myself.

I thought of all the benefits I'd reap from being the one to track down this laptop, and I followed my intuition. I looked at my rings and my hands again and kept tapping the table, bringing back the memory of the day I took this important picture. I had to get this picture out and in the hands of the law. Like right now.

Mr. Ziff was on his computer, writing an email to someone, and I asked if I should bring my phone with this picture into the office. I was so into my head that I couldn't recall if I actually had asked him aloud or in my head.

"I've been taking pictures, and I think this may be the guy who took the laptop, you know, number twenty-four." I showed him the picture. He looked at it blankly; it appeared he was mostly looking at his computer screen.

"I know you want to help, but what evidence do you have?" he asked.

"I'm pretty sure this guy in the picture is the same one that I've seen around campus looking suspicious on the weekends. I think I should alert Ms. Photenhauer and Mr. Arnold."

Mr. Ziff, smiling in a halfway sort of rhinoceros smile, said, "Do what you need to do, Frances. I suppose you can share this picture with them, but you don't have names or phone numbers."

He seemed a little annoyed with me. This wasn't what I was hoping for. I had an idea.

"Don't visitors have to sign in when they come to school?" I asked. I tried to sound as smart and calm as I could.

He agreed, nodding his head, and added, "There is a sign-in binder at the front desk."

"I'm on this, sir; be back in a bit." I took the library pass and walked outside.

I texted Abby, but I knew she was in PE and wouldn't answer. I was going to ask her if she thought the picture matched the guy we saw on the dog walk. I had zero time to waste.

I went straight to the principal's office. She was also on the computer writing something. I knocked even though the door was open.

"May I see the visitor sign-in sheet? I think I may have a lead on the missing laptop from the Innovation Center."

She told me she'd be there in a minute. "How is everything going for you, Frances?" she asked as she took a sip from her coffee cup, walking with me to the front desk in the office. She started to talk to one of the secretaries, so I held off on my answer. She handed me a thick white binder.

I flipped through until I saw January dates. "Excuse me, when did the Wednesday Academy Cartoon Animation class start?" I asked the secretary.

The principal was back in her office. I guess I didn't get her too excited. I was told the date January 23, the day the Cartoon Animation class started when the semester changed. I guess I could also ask Elijah, the teacher, but that would have to wait. Nobody had signed into the Innovation Center as the room they were visiting on that day. A couple of student teachers, a volunteer math tutor, and a lady named Shirley Carlisle who was helping with the Parent Teacher Club. That was it. I went back to the library and emptied out my pictures onto one of the student desktop computers using one of the cords. I sent the picture of evidence to myself on my student account and printed it. Crap, it was only a black and white, but at least I had the original on my phone. I stared at the picture until my eyes crossed. It was making me exhausted.

Mr. Ziff was doing something for our closed-circuit TV programs, and other than putting some books on a cart for me to put back on the shelves, he seemed to forget that I was ready to crack the code. I felt anxious. It was Thursday, and I wouldn't see Elijah until the following Wednesday. No, this couldn't wait. I took my phone and the picture I printed out, even though it was very poor in quality, and later tried to find Mr. Arnold. The door was left ajar, and I saw some eighth-grade girl I recognized. She was crying as he was showing her a printout of her grades. At least that's what it looked like. Sometimes I'm so observant I drive myself batty because my overactive brain is always working. Always. Night and day. Rain or shine.

"We'll be a few minutes, Frances, can this wait?" he said to me.

I told him, "It's important, but I can wait," and started to sit down on the bench to wait my turn. He walked out with this girl a few seconds later and said quietly, "Alondra, it's your job to bring up your grades. Start coming to homework club." He ushered me into his office. I felt like a robot by this point.

"You know the missing laptop, number twenty-four, well, I think I have a lead," I began. I showed him both pictures of the man and told him that nobody had signed in to be in the Innovation Center. "Yet here was this picture of two men in that room."

I added, "He hangs out around school on the weekend. I should know; I live close by." For some reason, I suddenly sounded like my grandma. She says things like, "I should know." Maybe it's the Jewish blood in me.

He was writing things down on a bright yellow pad attached to a clipboard. I wondered what he was writing. I also wonder what Joanie writes about me in therapy.

He said, "I'll call Elijah and see if he knew these men."

He thanked me for being an enthusiastic student and then took a close-up of my picture on the phone with his phone and told me that I was a stellar citizen or something like that. I couldn't sleep that night. Abby had plans with some other friends and didn't text me back. I told my mom at dinner that I just knew that this man in the picture was up to no good, and she seemed to be only half-listening. I showed her pictures from my phone, but she just zoomed in on Ingrid's face and kind of rolled her eyes. Ingrid really is pretty. It must bug my mom. It bugs me too.

I did my homework and then begged my mom to go to the gym for a swim.

"Oh, Frances, I'm too tired. One of my clients had a crisis, ran late, of course, and it threw off my day. I'm really sorry," she said, putting the leftover pizza and asparagus back into the fridge.

I managed to talk her into walking me to the gym, pretending she would work out, and then ditching out. It's that stupid no-minors-without-an-adult rule, but usually people think I'm in high school anyway. I just felt like swimming. It always clears my head. My mom went back and forth about wanting to stay at the gym and swim with me, but then her hair would be wet, and she was tired and didn't want to change out of a wet bathing suit, *but then on the other hand*, we hardly see each other, she really *does* need the exercise, blah, blah, blah…

Why can't that woman just make up her mind? I don't have the patience for wishy-washy. Why can't people come to a decision and stick to it?

We walked into the gym together, signed in, and walked straight into the ladies' room. I told her to come back in an hour and that I'd be fine. She left, mumbling about something, and I was actually relieved when she left. When I entered the swimming pool area and grabbed the swim noodle, I felt instant gratification that I could just disappear into the water, so that was exactly what I did.

At the gym I did laps and thought about my life: my dream of giving swim lessons, the many poetry books I'll write, how my husband will cut red and yellow roses from our rose bush for me every week, what my kids will look like, etc. I held my breath for as long as I could, staring at my blue and white polka dot swimsuit under the water.

I kept on thinking about my mom plowing into the car in front of us. Why do I keep on thinking about it? I hated that sound, but it comes back to me so easily, almost as if it's demanding my full attention. I noticed that Joanie wrote something on her clipboard when I told her that I keep hearing that sound of my mom's car crashing. Today had been a long day, after all. I wasn't appreciated for all the wisdom that I have, or for my psychic abilities. I was tired, really drained.

Thirty-Two

SEVENTH GRADE SEEMS LIKE A LONG way away, and it's taking like forever to complete sixth grade. I can't believe it isn't over yet. I'm not trying to brag or be mean, but I feel too mature to be in middle school. I don't fit into this picture. The students are boring. Abby is clearly my favorite, and I do like Kylie, the blonde girl who spent the night at my house and likes to sing with her uke (she is also super good in art and basketball), but the rest of the students are just background noise. I'm ready for a creative kind of high school with indigo friends, or even college.

I got tired of waiting for the principals to help. The vice principal was busy whenever I asked him, and it seemed that everyone just accepted that the Chromebook #24 was going to remain "missing." Frances didn't go for that.

I ended up asking my Wednesday Academy Cartoon

Animation teacher myself if these guys in the picture looked familiar. I went to class a few minutes early, watching Elijah, the teacher, get things ready for our class. He was humming as he turned on all of the computers. He was pushing the tables together with one hand, looking at his cell phone with the other. I asked him if he heard any updates. He told me he hadn't, only that it had been missing for a while.

Next, I talked to our school resource officer. He comes to our school a lot. He is very friendly and helpful. His name is Officer Ramirez. He talks to students about gangs, safety, drugs, making good choices, etc., and hands out stickers and comes to our assemblies and fundraisers. I pulled him aside a few days before school started. It was a few days before the eighth-grade graduation.

"I know you're busy, but I think I saw some foul play and I have a picture of who I think may have taken one of the school computers." We were standing out by the basketball hoops.

He was really grateful and asked more questions, and also asked to see the picture. I had it in a page protector in my backpack, very neatly placed in a red folder. Without blaming our principals, I just added that everyone figured we would not see the computer again, and let it go, but that I had a hunch and live close to the school. "What's more," I added, "I've seen this same suspicious person."

He took my copy of the pictures and also looked

at my phone. He said, “Thanks, I’ll definitely look into it.” He seemed a bit confused at first, as he was not completely aware of a missing laptop. “Nothing has been reported to me yet,” were his words.

The following day was the day before the last day of school. Mr. Arnold saw me standing in line at brunch. I wasn’t really hungry, but I thought a bagel and cream cheese sounded good. He told me, “Please go to your next class, and after roll gets taken go straight to my office. I will let Mr. Lammerding know that we need to discuss some things. I just don’t want you to be marked tardy or absent,” he said and sort of yawned. For some reason, he didn’t seem glad to see me like he usually does. I took one bite of my bagel, feeling it sink to the bottom of my stomach.

I went to my math class and let the teacher know I had to go to the office. Stupid ol’ Miles rolled his eyes. We both ignore each other, but this is how we usually greet each other, if at all. People were signing each other’s yearbooks and I saw roses in the office for the next day’s graduation. The ladies in the office were busy. Nobody seemed to notice me. After what seemed to be a long time, the vice principal walked over to the bench and nodded for me to follow him. He took the pictures I had placed in the page protector out of a file in his cabinet by his desk. He let out a sigh and scratched his head. “Well, young lady, good eye on one account. The pictures you have are of a real person. We have identified the person. I understand you even got Officer Ramirez involved. Oh, Frances, you meant well…"

He paused; I couldn't tell where all of this was leading. I knew there was more.

He was wiping a pen mark off his left index finger. "The problem, Frances, is that this person happens to be Peter's brother. He helps Peter. He wasn't doing anything wrong, in other words."

My face became hot. I heard clanging noises. Inside of my head was a bowling alley on a busy Saturday night.

"Peter?" I meekly squeaked out. "Who is Peter?" I quickly flashed on Peter Parker from Spiderman.

At that instant, he pushed open his office door and from the chair I was sitting on, I saw Peter. Peter is our custodian. I automatically recalled very similar posturing from the man I'd noticed and taken pictures of and Peter. Peter was dumping some paper into the recycle bin near the staff room. They both have shaved heads. I kept seeing even more family resemblances, and at the exact moment I connected the two, I felt silly. No, not silly, dumb. Idiotic. A freak. It gets worse. I felt glad to be in the privacy of the vice principal's office. I couldn't bear the thought of being in math class taking notes right then.

These were the words from Mr. Arnold, the man who used to like me: "The laptop that was missing was accidentally checked out to a retired teacher who needed it for some assembly, and apparently nobody at our site was aware that it was accounted for. Mystery solved."

I froze. I think he said something about having to leave to watch a teacher for an evaluation or something. The vibe was that he was busy, and I should exit his office.

And just like that, I felt a rain cloud of shame drench me. I was watchful for nothing. I didn't expect to, but I started crying. Mr. Arnold gave me a tissue and whispered, "You did nothing wrong. You were looking out for your school, hon. This is why you're so good at ASB"

This made me cry harder. I was glad he called me *hon*; it meant he didn't hate me, perhaps, but I know he was at least very disappointed in me. I failed. He left the office and came back with Peter, who had a trash can liner in his hands. Peter introduced himself, taking off his glove from his right hand. I told him I was sorry. I guess someone, either Mr. Arnold or Officer Ramirez, had left the picture of Peter's brother (Elian) somewhere, and Peter asked about it. Elian had been helping Peter clean out and fix old hardware from the Innovation Center and just happened to be fixing the lock on the Chromebook cart the day I snapped the picture.

Peter said, "No worries," a few times, but I just felt awful. All I had done was embarrass myself.

School was out for summer the next day. I told Joanie the whole story, from beginning to end. We were both quiet for a minute or two. She wrote things down, and I wiped my eyes. The sort of shameful feeling was oddly similar to me trying to give Mr. Ziff the dog Selma. We discussed the possibility that perhaps I'm trying too hard.

She asked me, "What do you really want, Frances?"

I was drinking tea and cream and looking out of the window. I felt like I was wasting her time and my mother's money. I must look like a fraud. I watched people walk by; a man was sitting on a rug playing guitar, a mother pushing a double stroller. I watched life passing by. I was in a daydream, as always.

"I want, I want..." I started. I remember letting some time pass because I really wanted to feel the inside of my stomach in order to answer her question. I know what it's like to be mindful. It basically means to pause, to not react right away. I saw a picture of me, of what I might look like at about twenty-two years old, getting my BA at a college graduation. I'm a grown up and on my own. My dad is applauding for me, and my mom and many friends are there standing up and clapping wildly. I realized I wanted to fast-forward my life. "I want to grow up," I finally said, stating it firmly.

Joanie looked at me straight in the eye, smiled in a gentle way, and wrote something down.

"Please repeat to me what you just said."

"I want to grow up," I repeated.

"Then stay where you are on this very path, because you're on the way, young lady. No need to rush anything." I swear Joanie said these words without blinking or taking a breath. She has one of those super expressive faces that you can't forget. Those words stayed with me:

No need to rush anything.

I feel like I'm getting a lot of lessons now. I'll be thinking about my dad or a store I remember in Boulder, and just then I'll see a Colorado license plate. I'm enjoying my time at home with the dogs now that school is out.

There is a lady down the street named Peggy who rescued this strange-looking white terrier Jack Russell mix. His name is Rudy. Sometimes we walk together. She invited me to the beach with our rescue dogs. She collects seashells and sea glass and makes art out of them. She's the parking attendant near this restaurant in front of the beach I like. She makes me laugh. She has really cute grandsons. One is four and one just turned a year old. Her husband is an Uber driver and also works with high school kids who get into trouble. He walks Rudy too, but the dog is crazy about Peggy. I once saw her rubbing her eyes, and an eyelash had gotten inside of her eye. I put my hand on her forehead to take it out, and Rudy acted like he was going to bite me.

I think rescuing dogs is so important to do. We bring blankets to the SPCA sometimes, and I think I'll volunteer to give the dogs walks and baths. I also have a few babysitting jobs lined up. I survived sixth grade at a new school in a new state. I really liked getting to know Hector and Ezra, who served on leadership and ASB Hector taught me some words in Spanish, and I'm pretty sure we'll hang out over the summer. Ezra plays drums, and who knows? Maybe if I get better with my piano chops, I can try out for his band.

I'm trying not to be so negative about kids my age. Hector is reading a book called *The Man Who Knew Too Much*. What a cool title, right? I want to start reading more.

Thirty-Three

ABBY AND KYLIE SPENT THE NIGHT last night. This is the second time Kylie has been over to my house. We had a pizza delivered, and Gary dropped us off at the roller rink. Kylie looked up on YouTube how to braid ethnic hair and offered to give me a makeover. We decided we would go in alphabetical order, so Abby was first on the chair. We actually took turns sitting on the bathroom counter. Kylie and I used a straightener on Abby's hair, and then took her longest strands on both sides and curled them dramatically.

With Abby still on the counter as our client, I told her to close her eyes. I ran as fast as I could to the freezer, bringing three coconut popsicles and paper towels. I shoved it in her mouth, unwrapped one for me, and handed the other one to Kylie.

Abby was licking the sides of her popsicle and asked us if we ever smelled our belly buttons.

Kylie and I told her she was nuts, and she said, "If we're really the Three Musketeer Middle School Best Friends, we all have to smell our belly buttons!"

We thought it was so weird, and then Kylie tried to get into a yoga pose to reach her belly, but of course it didn't work. Abby looked inside the vanity above her and found three Q-tips. She stuck the Q-tip in her belly button and made us smell it. It was nasty.

Don't tell anyone, but we agreed we all had to do it, and so we did.

I can't describe the smell. Maybe old minestrone soup that was left in a hot car.

Even though I don't wear makeup, Ingrid gave me a cosmetic bag a few years ago filled with samples and things that I'd never even unpacked or looked through before this time. I put eyeliner on Abby, and Kylie applied blush and some shiny watermelon lipgloss. I think she looked bomb. She's so adorable. Anyway, my hair turned out looking pretty good. I usually just let it go. When Kylie braided my hair, she used tiny little purple bands.

Have you ever just stared at yourself in the mirror until you can't even recognize yourself? Well, I just stared and stared, kind of leaving my body. I didn't know if I was in Boulder or California. I didn't know if I was a relative of Kevin Green or Harriet Goldstein, or if I was a blonde sister of Kylie's or even a strange model that Abby's mother would draw. I was a stranger out with my two friends, getting my hair done, and would soon be skating. I think I'm learning to live in the moment, like Joanie tells me. She says, "Try to notice if you can stay present, not looking for any certain outcome."

I decided that because I made it through a school year somewhat successfully, it was now time for Frances to reinvent herself. I liked looking at my cheekbones and my eyebrows in the mirror. I am, maybe, kind of pretty. Just a little.

At the roller skating rink, we all held hands and skated really fast. I saw Ezra and Phoenix, and when they passed me, they patted my head and Ezra said, "Looking sharp, Frances." It made me really happy. I licked my lips and thought that the watermelon gloss was helping this new thing, this new chapter in my life. I tried skating backward and wiped out, but luckily I clutched onto Kylie who grabbed onto some kid. We all grabbed the railing at the same time, but kind of twisted into a big pretzel and wiped out. You had to have been there, but trust me, it was crazy funny.

Some random guy with slicked-back brown hair and sunglasses on his head skated over to me and asked me to dance. It was that song by Celine Dion, "My Heart Will Go On," you know, from the movie *The Titanic*. He told me that his name was Dan and he is homeschooled. When we skated, it was loud and I was sweaty. We held hands. Dan has medium-sized soft hands. He asked for my number at the end of the night, which I gave him, but then he left with a middle-aged man and a couple of kids who stood impatiently by the door, motioning to him to hurry up. I could easily crush on him.

Thirty-Four

MY LIFE IS A WHIRLWIND. The teeter-totter goes up, and then it comes down. I get a nasty pimple on my chin, and just when I think that people are looking at it, I hear, "You're so lucky to have the curly hair you do."

I like compliments; I mean, really, who doesn't? The thing is, it throws me off when I'm thinking something dark about myself, and just then someone has their flashlight on me, telling me something that makes me feel that I shine.

Frank and I were baking chocolate chip cookies when my cell phone rang. The nice lady Leslie who lives down the street called. She asked me to babysit a group of kids, either three or four kids for sure, possibly five. The date was set for Sunday, July 26, to be exact. The babysitting job was supposed to start at dinnertime and end by 10:00 p.m. My mom had plans to walk with some work friends and then go out to dinner, but she said she could drop me off about 5:00 p.m. This resort where the babysitting job was at is called the Chaminade, and it's only a few miles from my house. I looked at the website and was happy to see a big pool by the tennis courts. One of the parents of the kids called me on Saturday and asked if I could start babysitting earlier on Sunday. Her name was Ellen and she also works at the hospital where Leslie does, only she is one of the head administrative people, or something like that. This get-together was for some celebration for the employees of the hospital. Leslie wasn't going to be there, and she just gave my name as a possible childcare provider.

So anyway, Ellen told me that she'd be happy to pick me up and meet my mom and bring me to the Chaminade to make things easier. She said she had a little girl who was seven months old and a boy named Tommy was just turned two years old. I could hear a little kid crying when she called the next day to inform me she was running a little late, but we'd hang out at the pool for a while. I kept on saying, "What? I can't hear you!"

She sounded apologetic that I couldn't hear her clearly on the speakerphone. When she pulled up in her Toyota Highlander, I was watering the succulents on the porch and giving my mom her cell phone contact information. Ellen had one hand on the steering wheel and with her other hand she was putting a little binky in her daughter's mouth. A little boy, Tommy, was holding an iPad mini and playing a game. Little kid music with clapping sounds was playing on the stereo, and the mom's cell phone was ringing. I was in a quiet mood, and kind of wished that I knew one of the parents. I was looking forward to making money and was hoping to journal between 5:00 and 6:00 p.m. when the job was supposed to start. This was when I thought my mom would be dropping me off. We introduced ourselves, and she shook my hand and also my mom's. It was warm but a little windy outside. She tried to get Tommy to say hello to me, but he was shaking his head and saying, "No," which seemed to tick her off.

"I promised to let him play in the pool, but I don't think we have time. We are members of Chaminade and use the pool pretty often. I have to be the greeter and get our banquet room ready," she said, again in an apologetic tone.

Tommy said, "I swim," with a lisp. He had a really cute smile and big brown eyes like a deer. He had very long eyelashes and a bright green shirt with an alligator on it.

I said, "I love to swim too, Tommy," and he finally looked at me. I told Ellen that another time we could swim.

Her phone rang again and she answered it, this time rolling her eyes. "Wait a sec," she said to the person she was talking to, and then she started twirling her hair. "Do you want to take this monster swimming for about fifteen minutes while I get things ready?" she asked.

I already had a bag packed with crayons, paper, the movie *Finding Nemo* on my laptop, two Dr. Seuss books, and Legos. "I'll grab my swimsuit and a towel and I'll be ready in a minute," I said. The idea of swimming always appeals to me. Because I know where everything is at all times, my swimsuit was on the towel rack. I grabbed it, put my key and cell phone in my backpack and said goodbye to my mom. I got in the front seat and buckled up. Her car was messy but not as bad as my mom's. She asked me if I had been to the Chaminade before, and I told her it was my first time. She seemed sweet, like a really caring mom. She looked about thirty-five years old. Her sunglasses were Gucci and she was wearing a yellow dress with a white shawl over it.

Tommy started kicking my chair. I could tell this kid was a handful. The little girl, Sasha, was sleeping like an angel. We parked and I stayed in the car as Ellen took a few bags into a big building near the entrance of this hotel/resort place. The valet guy kept asking if he should park the car, and I told him, "No," but he seemed confused. I felt uncomfortable; it seemed like Ellen left me in the car with her kids I hardly knew for a long time. I couldn't understand everything her little toddler said, but it was something about his dog, I think. He liked my rabbit foot keychain on my backpack, so I let him hold it. Ellen jumped back into the car and we parked by the pool. Ellen picked up Sasha and I helped Tommy out of his car seat. She opened the gate of the pool area and put that little lifesaver tube thing around Tommy's body. I changed into my swimsuit in the bathroom at the pool and then walked Tommy carefully to the steps of the pool. He held on to my hand very tightly. He was so excited! Ellen put a towel over her chest and was nursing Sasha, and once again, she was on her phone. She waved to us and Tommy said something like, "Hi Mommy, I have fun in da pool."

I showed him how to make bubbles and how to kick. He stood on the edge of the pool and jumped into my arms, splashing and laughing. I towed him around as he was kicking. I could tell he liked me.

Fast-forward to about fifteen minutes later. We dried off, changed back into our clothes, and walked back to the main building where Ellen had dropped things off. She showed me a small room on the second floor where I would let the kids draw and we would watch *Nemo* and just hang out. Ellen said they were going to bring us dinner at about 6:00 p.m. She was putting flowers in vases and signing cards while Sasha was asleep in her little carrier. I was told that the other kids were coming later.

Some lady who smelled like wine and strong, flowery perfume introduced herself to me and started touching my hair. Her name was Lupe and she was from Argentina. She said she wanted to take a walk and see the grounds, and asked if I could go with her. Tommy was playing with my bag of Legos and said, “Me go too.” Lupe was expecting her husband and daughter to come pretty soon, she said. The three of us walked to the pool, as Ellen had given me the pool key. It was weird; the key was just like a credit card. We all walked in, and it seemed many more people were at the pool. There was a cabana and some guy with a white shirt was selling drinks. Lupe bought a glass of wine and got me something that tasted like a cross between a Sprite and lemonade. It wasn’t very good, but I wanted to be polite.

Lupe waved to a car outside of the fence and told me to come out to the parking area. Her husband and daughter pulled up with a new, sparkling blue, Tesla and she showed me how it opens up like a spacecraft. Her husband showed us the car, and I got introduced to him and also their daughter, who was about six years old. She knew Tommy and they were playing on the grass outside of the pool. The little girl whose name I can’t even remember now walked away with her dad and they took Tommy with them. They came back a few minutes later, and Ellen walked over and put a jacket on Tommy. She had her baby Sasha in a stroller and was with another lady and her little boy.

We all sat down in the pool area, and Lupe was asking me about my family, what my nationality was because she said my skin and hair were so pretty. She seemed a little too friendly and also a little tipsy. She told me she liked me and passed me her phone, asking me to take a picture of her and her husband and this other lady who had just shown up. They were posing by the hot tub area. It was just starting to get dark.

I was trying to figure out the right button to take a picture on her phone when suddenly a shrieking scream was heard. The little girl, Lupe's daughter, who was with her dad, let out the worst bloodcurdling scream ever.

Lupe yelled, "Oh my God," as I saw Ellen drop to the ground. Her heels and yellow dress were all I could see for sure. Someone yelled, "Call 911, *now*!" and the next thing I saw, to my horror, was Tommy in the middle of the pool. He was thrashing around as Lupe's husband was trying to grab him. Some kids were in the pool screaming, and it was hard to tell what was going on. Without thinking it through, I remember dropping Lupe's phone on the ground and diving into the water. My instincts made me swim as fast as I could. Goal—grab Tommy—grab that little guy.

Someone else must have dove in because water was splashing everywhere, and I felt someone kick me under water. I saw Tommy's little black and orange Giants jacket, and the only things going through my head were hurry the hell up, focus, and do CPR. In that order. Hurry the hell up, focus, and do CPR. When I scooped him up, I got a mouthful of water and started burping. I was able to grab the small section of his back and place him on the cement.

Although people were yelling and maybe crying, someone handed me a towel and I repositioned him over the table to keep him warm. Somebody threw me a blanket. Lupe's husband was keeping people away so we had room. I think in the background I heard Lupe yelling, "Oh my God, please save this little boy. Oh my God!"

I checked for a pulse and was sure he didn't have one, but because I felt panicked, and I wasn't certain. The CPR manual popped into my head, and I turned him on his side. His eyes were closed but his body was thrashing around. A bunch of water came out of his mouth and he threw up. It stunk. I started compressions and just kept on going. Push. One, two, three, four, five. My hands were on top of each other, and though I know I was shaking, I made strong and deliberate thrusts. He had a tiny little chest, but I continued.

Someone yelled out, "Do you need help?" but I couldn't answer. It felt like a dark frenzy that was starting to get light. I could feel movement in his body, like he was waking from a terrible dream. I stayed focused, and I gave more compressions. I pinched his nose, giving him a few of my breaths. I exhaled fast, just a few times. It sounded like I was in a tunnel. His chest thrust upward and I heard a gasping sound. I realized he was breathing when I saw his chest rise, so I stopped. He was still coughing up more water, and a few pieces of throw up were coming out. His body was moving around like crazy, but I stayed calm and forced him to remain on his side. His mom was there, also holding him so he'd stay on his side.

He started crying and yelled, "Mommy!"

At this point, Ellen grabbed him and started rocking him gently. Someone from the Chaminade brought a bunch of towels. A fire engine came quickly and they checked him out. While Ellen was talking to one of the firefighters, another firefighter placed a weird-looking helmet thing that looked like a bubble over Tommy. I looked around the pool area to get my bearings and noticed Tommy had a blanket draped around his body and was now on a stretcher. He looked dazed and tired. The emergency lights were still flashing, and I heard people talking on radios. I remember shaking and stuttering when they asked me my name, age, and address. I thought I was going to throw up myself.

That lady Lupe started hugging me, and a bunch of people from the Chaminade asked me if I needed a robe or food or anything. My backpack was on the ground and the other bag I brought was in the other building, but at the time I just thought about my cell phone and house key, which were both in the backpack. I felt nauseated and I wanted to go home. An ambulance came, and by now the whole pool area was lit up with the lights from both emergency vehicles. The sound was off, but those lights were like a bad dream.

I remember Ellen telling me that Tommy was okay, but they decided to take him to the hospital for observations. She hugged me while one of the firefighters was holding Sasha. They left with Tommy on the stretcher. A firefighter wearing a helmet and a big yellow jacket told me he would take me home. They asked to talk to Mom or Dad. I gave them my mom's number because I was still kind of stuttering and was shaking too much to look for my phone. This was my first ride in a fire engine. I sat in the front with a female firefighter named Laurel. She said, "Great job, Frances. You saved that little guy. Get some rest."

My clothes were soaking wet. They put a thick, gray wool blanket on me. We got to my house and the first thing I saw was my grandma looking out of the window. She looked scared to death. She ran out to greet us. Laurel got out of the truck and told her to make me a hot shower or bath and stay with me. I usually take long baths, but all I could do was turn on the hot shower and stand there for a few minutes. I felt numb. I watched the chain of events unravel like I was watching a movie. I kept worrying that I did something wrong when I grabbed Tommy, but I swear it happened so freaking fast.

I wanted to text my dad since my mom wasn't home, but I just dried my hair and had the dryer on full blast. I needed heat. I was completely dry, but I kept staring at my shaking body and kind of spaced out with the dryer going at full power. I just played and played and replayed the scenes from the pool area. I kept thinking of Tommy, hoping he was okay. I thought about how he had a lifesaver ring around him and was jumping in my arms a few hours ago, so how did this happen? His mom was there, so I guess it wasn't my fault, but I felt guilty somehow. I couldn't get that CPR manual out of my head. My grandma came into my room afterward and lay down with me. Tommy's cute laugh and smile were haunting me. We were *just* laughing and playing. Everything was going so well. I thought of that putrid smell of puke. The light brown stripes on the Chaminade towel. Tommy floating on top of the water with his little Giants jacket on.

And then somehow, the sun rose the next morning.

Thirty-Five

MY MOTHER TOLD ME LIKE forty-seven times how sorry she was that she wasn't home when little Tommy Argos almost drowned. She said she decided to only work a half-day and wasn't expected to come in until after lunch. She looked at me as though she was waiting for me to say something, but I remember feeling private, like I wanted to stay inside of my head and heart.

I like the word *surreal*. It might sound odd, but the best way to explain it is that my stomach was rumbling. I kept thinking I had to use the bathroom, so I'd go in there, try to have a bowel movement, and then, well…nothing would happen. I'd walk back to the kitchen table, and then she'd start with the questions. My mother seemed to be stalking me.

My mother: "Franny, I'm here for you. Wanna walk? Talk? Go to the beach?"

Me: “Nope. Thanks.”

I think we repeated this conversation at least five times as we took turns opening the fridge and taking out slices of cheese and putting it on crackers. Nervous energy seemed to be making the paint peel off the walls. Frank was at work, so it was only the two of us at home.

I was in the bathroom when the dogs started barking as someone rang the doorbell. I heard someone say “Ellen” in a male voice. I peered from behind the bathroom door.

My mom let a tall and kind of handsome man inside. He was all dressed up in a gray shirt with a tie and khaki-colored pants. He was holding a bouquet of fresh red and yellow roses with baby’s breath, all wrapped up in white tissue paper. He sat on the couch with my mom, and five minutes or so passed. I realized he had the same smile as Tommy. I still stood by the bathroom door, watching all of this.

My mom kept calling my name, but I pretended not to hear her. I could hear only a little of the conversation. My mom kept saying, “It isn’t necessary.” She called my name again, so I flushed the toilet even though there was nothing to flush, let the faucet run for a minute, and then made my way to the living room with very slow and careful steps.

The man stood up, extended his hand as if he wanted to shake hands, and then he quickly hugged me. His back seemed wet, and he had gigantic sweat marks under both armpits. I sat down next to him, watching him pick up the bouquet and a small card addressed to me with cursive writing. He kept on pushing his short brown hair back. He kind of had that spiky hair that smelled good from the gel or hair product that he used. He said, "I'm Peter Argos, the father of a very lucky little boy named Tommy. Frances, we just can't thank you enough…"

My mother put her hand on my knee. "Franny, I told Peter that you love children and were glad to help, but he came by because—"

Peter cleared his throat and cut her off mid-sentence.

"On behalf of Ellen and our family, the least we could do is pay you a visit and thank you in person. So please, accept this and know we will never forget you." He was speaking fast.

The dogs barked as the front door opened. Gary walked in with Frisbee and handed me a large Starbuck's chai with soymilk, just the way I like it. My mom introduced Gary to Peter, who apologized for staying so long. My mom told Gary to find a nice vase, and Peter handed me an envelope.

My mom said, "This isn't necessary."

Peter said, "Please, it's the least we can do. Frances saved our son's life." He looked like his eyes were beginning to tear up.

Gary, who is usually quiet, carefully placed the roses and the baby's breath in a tall red vase. He said, "Can I say something, Raych?"

The living room became quiet. All eyes were on Gary. "From what I hear, Frances did a very cool thing. If he wants to give her something, just let him."

I appreciated Gary's easy-going nature. My mom backed off, and I took the envelope.

I felt weird opening it in front of everyone, so I waited until Peter left. My stomach continued to rumble. I returned to the bathroom, nervous and shaky. I opened it.

The card had a picture of a cute Golden Retriever puppy sitting on a blanket on the beach with the caption, *Thank you for your kindness.*

My heart is pounding as I type this. In perfect cursive, written with a purple Sharpie, were these words:

Dear Frances,

We are at a loss for words to properly thank you for your fast thinking skills and courageous effort. Your bravery saved our precious Tommy, and we are eternally grateful.

Please use this small token of gratitude toward something special. God bless you, Frances.

Yours truly,

Peter, Ellen, Tommy and Sasha Argos

Inside of the envelope was…drum roll…a Target gift card and a check for $300.

Nothing like this had ever happened to me before. I told my mom I was feeling anxious. "Please make an appointment with Joanie for me. It always makes me feel better," I said.

It's a little embarrassing, but I still feel something like a lump in my throat when I go over the events at the pool. Like something is stuck between my face and my chest. I think about what would or could have happened if I had been looking at my phone or just wasn't paying attention.

Later that evening, I found out that Joanie was on vacation for ten days. I needed her.

I knew I could talk to Abby, but we didn't hang out as much as we used to. I didn't want her to think that I was bragging about getting all this money. I guess I could have called Kylie. But at that moment, my instincts told me to tune into myself and listen to what I wanted to do.

I started to read an old Harry Potter book from my bookshelf, but my mind was racing and I kept reading the same sentence three times. I made a cream cheese and cucumber sandwich and got on my bike. I rode straight to the beach, realizing that I forgot my cell phone on the kitchen table. When I sat on the sand, facing the crashing waves, I thought about the last few months of my life. I was sort of glad not to have my phone as a distraction. I didn't really want to talk to anybody, anyway. Well, only Joanie. So I pretended that Joanie was sitting next to me. She would likely ask me if I had been hanging out with friends since school let out. How would I answer? The word *weird* kept popping into the front of my brain.

How weird that I could feel so close to Abby one day, and then I didn't even call or text her to tell her about little Tommy Argos. How weird that I accidentally accused someone named Peter of taking a laptop, and then I met a kid, saved his life, and his dad's name was Peter. How weird that I historically get into trouble for pushing limits and taking things too far, and then I did the right thing at the right time, used CPR to help a drowning kid, and I was like a hero. How weird that I had Abby and Kylie over, and we all went skating and had fun with zero drama. Maybe things were getting better, maybe I was growing up. How weird.

I pulled out my leather-bound journal and decided to dig deeper.

> *In a funny way, it's like I took a very hard class, and I passed the test. I've figured out how to live my life. The thing is, I wanted so badly to be the hero with the missing laptop at school, and it was a terrible experience. I was the opposite of a hero. With Tommy, I just acted on impulse and did something great. Maybe all of my swimming*

experience helped. I want to quit trying so hard to be noticed and liked, sort of like getting Mr. Ziff a dog. To be honest, my biggest fear in life is that I'll be "average" and won't be known for any particular strength. Another fear is that I won't keep my friends because they'll get tired of me, or I'll get tired of them. I guess I need to do yoga poses more, you know, take deep breaths.

I want to be a writer one day. I want to live closer to my dad and not feel so annoyed with my mom. I want to stop hearing the sound of the car crash we got into. I want Frank to do fun things with me and talk about his feelings. I want to feel less anxious and laugh more. I want to go skating with Abby and Kylie and meet new friends. One day I want to have a boyfriend who'll read great books with me and challenge me with big words. I want to be kissed and loved. One day, I mean. Mostly, I want to practice being present, mindful, and not rushing anything.

I put the $300 check into my bank account, got a teen debit card, and bought a lamp, a lime-green trash can, and clothes from Target. My favorite new thing is a purple-and-black poncho. I wrote the Argos family a thank-you letter and have a date to babysit for them next week. I baked an apple pie and plan on bringing two pieces to my appointment with Joanie tomorrow. I miss seeing her; it has been twelve days since my last session. We'll eat pie together, and I'll tell her all about Tommy and the "Frances, The Lifesaver" event.

I can't wait, but I'll wait patiently. This is the new me.

It's now been a full year that I've been in Santa Cruz, California. My new life. The kind of life that makes me feel like I don't have to try so hard at it. The kind of life that will unfold on its own. The life I'm not rushing.

This time, Frances, you haven't gone too far.

A novel of a year in my life,
written by Frances Lily Green

The End

Frances, This Time You've Gone Too Far

About the Author

Janis Ost is a writer, mother, and middle school teacher. Passionate about writing with kids, especially adolescents, she is a writing project assistant with the Young Writers Program in Santa Cruz, California. She enjoys the quiet magic of sailing, playing the guitar, and encouraging people to be mindful. This is her second book, following *The Long Nights of Mourning* (2003).

Acknowledgments

With deep gratitude, I thank Brad Pauquette, Emily Hitchcock, Zoe Quinton and Joanne Hartman for their editing expertise, my writing instructors Robert Wilder and Margaret Wrinkle, Julia Chiapella and The Young Writers Program, my beloved teaching staff and former, present, and future students at Branciforte Middle School for the inspiration of Frances Green. Mind, body and spirit are one, so I include Cheri Bianchini from Healthy Way, Michelle Franklin for years of listening, John Lehr for guidance, Rhan Wilson and Pipa Pinon for teaching me about music, Daniel Jahangard and Brittany Birchall from Crossfit West in Santa Cruz, Clara Minor from Minorsan for keeping me strong and focused, my beloved kids Carina Ost, Cody Ford and stepson Ben Ford, Paul Horvat for making my heart fly, my dear sister friends, (you know who you are),

Julie Schneider, Joyce Blaschke, Chief Andy Mills and the dedicated officers, staff, and fellow volunteers at The Santa Cruz Police Department, and my loyal dogs, Stella, Tootsie and Bruno, for the unconditional love, neighborhood strolls and hikes.

My memories of being a student at Bowditch Middle School were fantastic. I must thank Mr. Ed Schuler, who treated our eighth-grade class like he cared deeply for each of us and encouraged me to write. Also, my sixth-grade besties Beth Burkhead Morris and Sophie Dupart, who gave me stomachaches from laughing so hard.

Everyone gets to the door
at different rates.

Wendy Thompson, stellar teacher and my wonderful colleague at Branciforte Middle School

CPSIA information can be obtained
at www.ICGtesting.com
Printed in the USA
BVHW072115310719
554781BV00002B/150/P

9 781633 372986